SPACE TRIP II

SPACE TRIP II
THE JOURNEY TO FIND THE SECRET OF THE THING IN THE BOX

NICK MARONE

Delta-V Press
Queanbeyan, New South Wales, Australia

First published in Australia in 2022 by Delta-V Press

Copyright ©2022 Nick Marone
nickmarone.com

ISBN: 978-0-6488641-4-1

A prepublication catalogue record for this book is available
from the National Library of Australia.

Cover art by Tom Edwards
tomedwardsdesign.com

Printed by Lightning Source

This book is dedicated to Isaac Asimov, H. G. Wells, and Timothy Zahn. Their stories ignited my interest in science fiction.

1

THE STRANGE BOX

The air swirled thick in the antique shop. It was an old and cramped building, filled with aged furniture and interstellar oddities, and it was precisely Dave Winkle's cup of tea. After travelling extensively on *Liberty*, becoming a resort city's new chief financial officer, and spending every day with his friends, Dave just wanted to rest. He resigned himself to being a hermit just as soon as he returned to Haven Resort on the garden world of Paradise, and there was nothing more hermit-like than *real* timber furniture, shelves of fragrant books with *actual* pages, and a good brown cardigan. He already had the cardigan.

The shop was not big, but there were so many little rooms to discover, each hiding new trinkets and secrets. Dave often lost his friend, James "Jimmy" Jonathon Jones, only to spot him again as the energetic Irishman trudged past a doorway or spoke louder than antique shop etiquette allowed.

The shopkeeper was an enthusiastic Bejeklan originally hailing from a quiet corner of the galaxy. He hovered around, casually watching Dave and Jimmy with multiple eyes on the ends of twirling Medusa-like tendrils. In reality, only Dave was seriously shopping. He had dragged Jimmy along while their friends Chuck P. Simpson and Eddie Harrison led an investor's meeting for the rebuilding of their newly acquired resort city. Jimmy made a good show of enjoying himself with the antiques.

Dave inspected a fading leather chair he knew would look perfect in his new house on the outskirts of Paradise Central. He planned to name his house The Hermitage. He ran his hand along the chair's smooth surface before dropping into it, the leather farting as he sunk into the plush cushion. He breathed a sigh and put his arms on the wide armrests. Yes, he could sit in that chair every afternoon while he relaxed from doing hermit stuff. From this throne, he surveyed the main room of the shop and felt truly at peace.

It was at this moment that Jimmy crossed Dave's field of vision, ruining said peace. The erratic man, freshly appointed as Haven Resort's marketing director, stopped at a wall reserved for sporting equipment from days gone by. Dave watched as Jimmy eyed all the old clubs, bats, racquets, gloves, and balls before picking up a powered tennis racquet that could have been a hundred years old. Tennis in its original form was a dying sport, still played only by the most pompous of prep school kids and business executives, but Jimmy had apparently seen or known enough of it to find an accompanying tennis ball and occupy himself.

What Jimmy didn't realise was that he had picked up one of the first models of powered tennis racquets ever produced. With the introduction of the Robotic Tennis League, officials saw the potential to make the sport more interesting. Thus, the powered racquet was born, a design that was completely identical to standard racquets, but which included a special power supply to add artificial power to the strings. This was deemed too dangerous for sentient players. Several incidents involving powered racquets—such as two players suffering concussions, one getting a broken wrist, and another catching a ball in her mouth at the expense of her front teeth—led to the banning of such equipment by the Galactic Tennis Federation. A new robot league became the sole exhibit for powered racquets, and eventually the normal game declined as audiences preferred the faster and more destructive version where robots would be smashed to bits by hardened tennis balls.

Back to the scene at hand. Jimmy, happy now that he had something with which to amuse himself, warned Dave to catch the ball that he would gingerly volley from the other side of the store. Dave sat in the chair shaking his head, wondering if the shopkeeper knew what was brewing.

Jimmy, ignoring the headshake, tossed the tennis ball up with gusto and then lightly swung the racquet in Dave's direction. But when the ball met the racquet's strings, a furious artificial force sent it flying across the room. Jimmy hadn't noticed the powered mode was active. Dave, with reflexes he attributed to his strict exercise regimen, screamed and pushed himself out of the way, toppling the leather chair. The ball crashed through a large vase on a table, shattering it, and then knocked over a carved pedestal supporting a wooden box.

Of course, the shopkeeper had entered the room just as the episode happened. His mouth twisted open and his multiple eyes blinked at the damage. Dave shook his head again before getting up, crossing the room in a few quick bounds, and snatching the racquet out of Jimmy's grip.

"I'll take the racquet," Jimmy told the shopkeeper with a nod. "And the pieces of that vase," he added, pointing to the mess at the other end of the room. "And that box on the floor."

"And the pedestal?" the shopkeeper asked.

"What am I going to do with a pedestal?" Jimmy replied, but the shopkeeper stared him down. "And the pedestal too."

The shopkeeper mumbled something in his alien tongue and waddled off to the paystation.

"Well, get over there and clean up your mess," Dave said. He deactivated the racquet's power mode and went for the simple wooden box that had sat so regally atop the toppled pedestal. But it was deceptively heavy. Dave was the strongest of his little group of friends—a fact he humbly kept quiet under loose-fitting shirts—but the weight of the thirty centimetre-square box surprised him.

"What's wrong?" Jimmy asked, watching. "Muscle man struggling with a little box like that?"

"Here, you have a go," Dave said, handing it to Jimmy. The Irishman tensed and his arms sagged when Dave dropped it in his outstretched hands.

The shopkeeper gave a harsh laugh from his counter. "That box is, indeed, heavy. It was donated by a random customer who I only saw once—a strange creature. She came in, placed it on the pedestal, and it hasn't moved since."

"Well now, what interesting goodies have I found?" Jimmy asked. He tossed it up and caught it, getting comfortable with

4

its weight and shape, then waltzed over to the shopkeeper at the counter.

Dave squinted and scratched his chin. "What's in it?"

"I don't know," the shopkeeper shrugged. "It won't open. And believe me, I've tried."

The shopkeeper handed them a magnifying glass that was probably older than all their ages added together. Jimmy inspected his loot. There was a fine join running all the way around the middle of the box, barely perceptible even with the aid of the magnifying glass. It was clearly the connection of two halves, but there were no archaic hinges, nor an old-fashioned lock or modern keypad or touchscreen. It was just a perfect wooden cube with something inside. Or nothing. It could have been hollow, or it could have been solid timber. It was a sort of Schrödinger's cat scenario: until Jimmy opened the box, he was simultaneously lucky and unlucky in his decision to purchase it.

Jimmy clawed at it, but to no avail. He shook it and smacked it, looking much like a skinny monkey trying to bash open a coconut. Defeated, he set it on the counter with a thud and waved at it so Dave's more meticulous eyes could inspect it. Dave put his hands on his knees and bent for a closer look.

"Go on, muscle man," Jimmy taunted, "crack it open like a walnut."

Dave arched his eyebrows and looked up at his friend. "This is a big walnut."

"The price is two hundred EsCes," the shopkeeper said.

Jimmy nearly choked. "Two hundred Standard Credits? Why so much?"

The shopkeeper's long eye tendrils danced around before aiming at Jimmy's face. "I don't know what's in it! The contents could be worth ten times that."

"And yet, there could be nothing in it at all," Dave said.

Jimmy turned to his friend. "Do you think it's worth it?"

"I don't know," Dave replied, ever in a quagmire of doubt. "I'm an accountant, so I am normally against such wasteful purchases. But I am curious to see if there really *is* something inside. You won't know until you find out."

Jimmy smiled, needing no more discussion. "I'll take it."

THE OTHER HALF OF our quartet of hapless adventurers busied themselves in a much more important activity. Half an hour away from the antique shop, on the top floor of a glass skyscraper in the busy city centre, Chuck P. Simpson and Eddie Harrison wore their best suits and smiles. Chuck had combed his hair into his usual perfect pompadour, while Eddie shaved his strands a bit shorter so he wouldn't have to comb them at all.

Lined up in front of them were half a dozen of the planet's wealthiest investors. They wore expensive clothes, their jewellery glittered against the room's natural light, and their high-quality colognes and perfumes tickled the nose. They were too rich for Eddie—an entirely different social group compared to his humble beginnings. Even though he became a millionaire towards the end of his twenties, he'd started in the slums of Greater Manchester and worked himself out of poverty through sheer hard work and, unfortunately, some criminal activity. Chuck, at one point the most highly sought-after barrister in London, was in his element, which was why they both agreed that Chuck should do the schmoozing.

"In conclusion," Chuck said, "Haven Resort—and, by extension, the planet Paradise—represents a golden opportunity for investment in the resort sector. Its natural beauty is a fine attraction. The ecology is unheard of. Its history is unique in the entire galaxy. And our eco-friendly reconstruction plans are a huge step forward in city planning. Haven Resort was a profitable location in the past, and it has the potential to draw in three times as much income according to our forecasts. You, as investors, are what we need to succeed. And we *will* succeed. And with that success comes a sizeable, regular return on your investment. All we ask is that you make the right decision. Thank you."

Chuck took a deep breath and turned off the projector. His last slide, a simplified line graph, flickered out. Eddie stepped forwards and shook Chuck's hand while the audience talked among themselves.

"Nailed it, mate," Eddie said, then cringed. "Now dry your hands before they seal the deal." He wiped Chuck's palm sweat on the side of his trousers.

"I don't like the look on their faces," Chuck said. He turned around and dabbed his hands on a handkerchief. "Something is wrong."

"You're just imagining the worst," Eddie told him. Between Chuck and their introverted friend Dave, it was hard to know who was more pessimistic sometimes. But Eddie had to admit that none of the investors seemed in any hurry to shake their hands and offer money. They all sat in their chairs, reading through preliminary reports or whispering to each other. He gulped. Chuck's pessimism was spreading to him already! Maybe they should have brought along the greatest spin doctor they knew: Jimmy.

Eddie cleared his throat, determined to stay positive. "Any questions?"

All six investors raised their hands.

Chuck turned around and raised his eyebrows. He pointed to the lady on the left end. "Ms Amidane."

"I am worried about the safety of this world," she said. "If what you say is true—that the original resort was destroyed by the planet's living, thinking vegetation—then how can we be sure that it won't happen again?"

"We have a signed agreement with the Emissaries of Paradise," Chuck said. He tried not to get flustered, because he had already explained this point earlier. "The planet suffered severe ecological destruction during the Green Rebellion and the Emissaries can only repair so much. The income from our tourist venture will help repair what nature cannot do alone."

"So part of the profits will go into the environment?" Amidane asked.

Chuck heard her tone. "Yes."

She dropped her head and made notes on a digipad.

"Mr Ragowicz?" Eddie asked, making sure to pronounce the Polish billionaire's name exactly as he was told by the man's assistant before the meeting.

"How insistent are you on rebuilding environmentally friendly?" Ragowicz asked. "The term you used was . . . 'walking lightly' or something."

"Touching the planet lightly," Chuck said. "Yes, we are *very* interested in blending our resort as much as possible into the planet's ecology. We will make the most use of passive design features, sustainable work practises, eco-friendly materials, and technological innovations to reduce pollution and other impacts on the environment."

"That will make this project quite expensive," Ragowicz mumbled.

"Hence the investment target," Chuck said. "But the expected return outweighs the initial investment."

"If the planet doesn't revolt again," Amidane said.

"If anyone dares to visit it again," said a tall, narrow-framed alien named Ebbe. "All your projections assume that tourists will *want* to return. And what are you doing for the families who lost relatives in the first disaster?"

Chuck felt himself getting overly warm and resisted the urge to tug at his collar. He felt so tiny in this meeting. It was a far cry from his heyday as London's top civil litigator when he'd dominate a courtroom with his presence alone. These people gobbled up interstellar businesses before breakfast.

"The Green Rebellion occurred while Haven Resort was under different management," Chuck explained. "We bought them out after the incident, but compensation is still their responsibility. None of those expenses have anything to do with us."

"But they do," Ebbe said. "I asked about families who had lost relatives. That is not limited to relatives who died. You said there are several hundred Emissaries on Paradise—people who were subsumed into the planet, who *became* the planet. I admit I was sceptical about the existence and nature of these Emissaries until we watched that introduction video by Chief Emissary Sequoia. Regardless, these Emissaries cannot leave the planet, because they are the planet, so their whole lives have changed. What about their families? What will their families want in exchange for losing their loved ones forever?"

"They haven't lost their loved ones at all," Eddie said. "The Emissaries are alive and well. They chose to be united with Paradise. Their families can come and visit them anytime they want."

"And we offer families of emissaries free passage to Paradise and free accommodation while they are on-planet," Chuck added. "It is the least we can do to help them stay in close contact with their plant-based relatives."

Amidane grunted. "More money lost."

The investors descended into a loud discussion, but from Chuck and Eddie's perspective, it sounded more like an opposing army ready to pounce. Chuck's heart sunk.

One of the investors who hadn't said anything for the whole meeting stood, shook Chuck and Eddie's hands, dried his now damp hands on his clothes, then apologised, saying that he would not be buying into Haven Resort. But he wished them luck before leaving the room. Amidane didn't bother saying goodbye at all. Ebbe and another investor offered suggestions on how to improve their project's chances of success, which mostly included stripping the requirements for ecological sustainability.

The sound of silence whistled in Chuck and Eddie's ears once everybody had left, and the odour of expensive fragrances lingered. It smelled of lost money.

"Three failed investment meetings in a row," Eddie said.

"Yep," Chuck replied.

"Where are we going wrong?"

"It's not us," Chuck told him. "It's these rich bastards who don't want to see some of their profits go into the environment." He pulled out his phone. "Dave sent me a message."

"What's it say?"

"Two seconds. I have to call Wayne first."

Wayne Harris was Chuck's long-time work colleague and the man whom Chuck had selected to inherit the reigns of his law firm. Harris was a senior partner when Chuck was owner and CEO of the firm, but since having his mid-life crisis and taking on the Paradise project, Chuck stepped down from his position as CEO and asked Wayne Harris to take over. Chuck still owned the company and served on its board of directors, but Harris now controlled much of its operations.

A shimmering 3D hologram of the bespectacled Harris grew out of Chuck's phone. "Wayne! Hope I'm not disturbing you."

"Not at all," Wayne replied groggily. His hair was a mess and he had bags under his eyes. He flashed one of his two signature smiles—the genuine one reserved for friends, not the one for clients, courtrooms, and boardrooms. "What can I do for you?"

"I need you to set up another investment meeting."

"How did today's meeting go?"

"Best not to ask."

"Ah. I'm sorry. Okay, I'll see what I can do. There is no shortage of investors in the galaxy. But it will wait until after I officially wake up. It's three in the morning here."

Chuck slapped his forehead. Without Dave's mathematical mind, he could never figure out interstellar time zones. There were enough apps and websites that could do the calculations for him, but if Dave wasn't around he preferred to wing it. "Sorry! And thank you, I appreciate your help."

"Anything for a friend."

When Chuck hung up, Eddie asked him what Dave wanted.

"Oh, yeah." Chuck looked. "He says Jimmy's bought a weird cube from an antique shop and that we should check it out. Reckons it's like nothing he's ever seen before." He showed Eddie a photo.

"It's certainly a cube. What's so great about it?" Eddie asked.

Chuck texted the question to Dave and got a reply seconds later. "It weighs a tonne and they don't know if anything is inside. They can't open it."

Eddie grinned, reached into his jacket pocket, and pulled out the solution to many of his problems. Yes, even while wearing a suit, he carried his favourite object in the galaxy— his screwspanhamulesawilevelplifench multi-tool.

2

HEADBUTTING THE WALL

I<small>T WAS THEIR GLAMOROUS</small> mobile base of operations—a grey watermelon-shaped vessel that ferried Chuck, Dave, Eddie, and Jimmy between the stars. They had named it *Liberty* because it granted them relative freedom and a break from their previously mundane lives, though those lives were far from mundane now. This ship had a soul, of sorts—a snarky, sassy soul. Eve, *Liberty*'s artificial intelligence program, ran the ship so the guys wouldn't die in the nether regions of space. Were it not for Eve, our forever ill-prepared band of adventurers would have imploded, starved, crashed, or burnt up ages ago.

"So let me get this straight," Eve said when Jimmy put the box on the dining table next to the galley. "You bought a wooden box without knowing what was in it, brought it onto the ship, and you want to open it right next to your food preparation area?"

Jimmy surveyed the pristine galley that Dave had cleaned before they went shopping. "Yeah."

"Have you lost it, man?" Eve asked. Her smooth robotic voice had just the right tone of condescension mixed with playfulness that the guys knew and loved.

"In our defence," Dave said, hands up, "this box is so fascinating. It's heavy."

"A sumo wrestler is heavy," Eve said. "Sumo wrestlers are fascinating. This is a box."

Jimmy shook his head. "This box is special."

Eve let the dull sound of the air filtration system punctuate her silence. "Well, my humanoid friends, now I want you to open it."

"We need Eddie," Jimmy said. "He'd be the only one to get it open."

"You're in luck," Eve told them. "Eddie and Chuck are pulling into the cargo hold now."

They waited as the elevator took half an eternity to go down one deck and another half to rise back up. A beleaguered Chuck and Eddie stepped out. Eddie already had his tie off, two buttons undone, suit jacket clenched unceremoniously in his left hand. Chuck looked two degrees more sullen than usual.

"Did we get funding?" Dave asked.

Chuck dropped into a dining chair. "Nope. Wayne's finding more investors for us." It was obvious that he didn't want to discuss it, because he quickly pointed at the cube in front of him. "So this is it?"

"Sure is," Jimmy said excitedly. "Try lifting it."

Chuck shot him a glance. He grabbed the box with both hands and grunted. "What's the gimmick?"

"No gimmick," Dave said. "The damn thing weighs more than it should. No timber box is that heavy by itself."

Eddie threw his jacket over a chair and had a go. "It feels like I'm lifting a car battery." He stepped away.

Dave clenched his fists, letting his biceps ripple. "Why don't we just smash it open?"

"Hey, no way!" Jimmy said. "I paid too much for this. We're not destroying it."

"Just how much did you fork out for this thing?" Chuck asked.

Jimmy zipped his mouth closed and tossed away an invisible key.

"Two hundred EsCes," Dave said.

Chuck's face contorted into something akin to disgust. "You wasted two hundred on this?"

"Mate, it was a stab in the dark," Jimmy reasoned, "a risk into the unknown. Like those people who buy abandoned shipping containers. Who knows what treasures are hiding inside?"

"It could be empty!" Chuck replied.

"But it could be full," Jimmy said. Then he uttered a phrase often repeated among his friends: "We won't know until we find out."

"Guys," Eddie called from behind them. They turned to look. He twirled the single greatest tool in the whole universe on one finger. His screwspanhamulesawilevelplifench shone under the galley's lights like a gift from God. "I know how to get this thing open."

Eddie approached the table and the guys parted like the Red Sea. Eve played an epic symphonic theme on the galley's speakers, the sort one would hear at the end of a movie when the hero returns to win the day despite insurmountable odds. Eddie stood over the box, studying its perfect surface. Then he methodically cycled through the tool's menu before selecting the right extension for the job—a utility knife. It grew out of the screwspanhamulesawilevelplifench's handle, morphing into a solid blade.

"I see no intricate joinery techniques, so it's probably just glued together," Eddie said. "Eve, cut the music, please."

Now in silence, he found a minuscule line that could have been the join of two halves and tried slipping the blade inside. He wiggled it and moved his hand back and forth, but the razor-sharp edge failed to bite. Wary of scratching the timber and earning Jimmy's ire, Eddie pocketed his tool and ran a hand over his short, thinning hair. "No go. Let me think about it." He sat at the table, folded his arms, and stared at the box. He had never been defeated so quickly by something so simple.

"Maybe it's voice activated," Chuck suggested. He leaned forwards. "Open sesame!"

"I highly doubt that's the phrase," Dave told him. "That shopkeeper said he didn't know what planet this box came from. That means we don't know what language to speak to it—if it *is* voice activated. I have a better idea."

Dave stepped into the galley, reached for a large cooking pan, and raised it high above his head.

"No!" Jimmy shouted, grabbing Dave at the wrist. "Get your ridiculously huge arm away from it! I said no damage." He pulled the pan out of Dave's hand.

"I could study the material," Eve said calmly. "Maybe I can learn its origins."

Jimmy gingerly picked up the box, avoiding Dave's muscles, and carried it to Eve's info panel next to the refrigerator. He held it in front of her optical sensor, turning it as she prompted.

"Yes," she said, "it's wooden."

Jimmy sighed and put the box on the galley bench. "This is pointless. Cameron! We need Cameron. Where are you, Mr Flying Encyclopaedia?"

Dave's hyperactive camera drone, a zippy yellow globe, flew into the galley. "Someone called for me?" His main camera lens swivelled to look at each man in turn.

"Yes," Jimmy said. "We need your knowledge. Where have you been?"

"Downloading free books from Project Stevenberg. How can I help?"

"Can you identify where this timber came from?" Jimmy moved the box from the galley bench to the dining table.

Cameron hovered closer and scanned it several times using different techniques. "There are no available records in the public domain that identify this timber, nor do any of my local files shed light on its origins. I can conclude, however, that it is hollow."

"Is anything inside?" Jimmy asked. His hands shook with excitement.

Cameron gave scanned it with another sonic pulse. "It is empty."

"How peculiar," Chuck mumbled.

Jimmy slapped a fist into a palm. "Impossible. We've got to open it! Eddie, have you thought of a solution yet?"

"No. These things take time."

"Not if you rush them."

"You don't want it broken," Eddie retorted, "so now I have to think."

Chuck stood. "Maybe we should take it to a xenologist."

"That's a good idea," Dave said.

"Yeah, yeah, now we're talking," Jimmy told them. "Let's put our brains together. Crack this puzzle."

"Brains?" Eve asked quietly in the background.

"All the best xenologists are on Earth," Chuck said. "The University of Oxford will be the place to start." He pulled out his phone and grinned. "I know that because I helped them gain access to an archaeological site many years ago. Their Xenology Department is out of this world, no pun intended."

Eddie held up his hands. "No pun appreciated."

Chuck shrugged off the comment. "There's no guarantee that anyone will know what this is, let alone where it came from or how to open it. It looks like nothing more than a wooden cube to me, or, as I like to call it, a waste of two hundred EsCes."

Jimmy slapped the galley bench. "Ha! Well, whatever's inside, I won't be sharing it with you."

"I think we should go back to that shopkeeper and ask him some questions," Dave suggested. "The more we know, the more we can tell a xenologist."

"Agreed," Eddie said. "The sooner the better. Plus, it'll be a nice break from unsuccessful investment meetings."

"Agreed," Chuck said.

Jimmy scooped up the box and dropped it into a nearby backpack. "Let's go. Chuck, we'll take your car."

"Of course we will. It's the only car we have."

IT DIDN'T TAKE LONG for the guys to add a personal vehicle to *Liberty*'s cargo hold. They had been using Chuck's Vogel sedan for a little while now. Chuck, who owned multiple vehicles on several planets, volunteered the car for several reasons: one, the colour was champagne, and he knew Jimmy hated that; two, it was comfortable enough to ferry four crazy men around whatever city they visited; and three, he really liked the hood ornament—a falcon poised for flight.

"Take care out there," Eve warned as they piled in.

"The last time I drove on these streets was ten minutes ago," Chuck said. He started the engine and heard the satisfying rumble of the deceptively powerful engine that was still warm from its last trip. "The local drivers have nothing on my skills."

"You didn't let me finish," Eve said. "A large flock of pyat birds is moving over the city. Sometimes they cause traffic hazards."

"Noted," Eddie said. "Thanks, Eve. We shouldn't be too long."

Jimmy sat in one of the back seats, drumming his fingers on the box to some improvised melody. "How fast can this thing go?" Jimmy asked.

"As fast as the speed limit," Chuck old him. "Now buckle up. You want the roof down?"

Jimmy and Dave shouted affirmatively, but Eddie said he'd rather not.

"Sorry," Chuck said. "Majority rules. Looks like you'll be losing more hair today."

Eddie shook his head while the others laughed at him. Eve opened *Liberty*'s cargo door and Chuck nudged the car out into the sunny afternoon.

Isthan was a truly alien world—a pale purple sky hung over a city of whitewashed buildings of strange parametric shapes. The spaceport was busy with workers and technicians, but there was barely a human in sight. The pure-blood Isthanese dominated all walks of life.

A cloud of skinny pyat birds soared slowly overhead.

"Hmm. Maybe we shouldn't have the roof down," Chuck said, eyeing the birds. He brought it back up. "Can you imagine the droppings from those things."

"Probably why the buildings are all white," Eddie surmised. He turned around and inspected *Liberty* as they drew away from her. He sighed. "Yeah, they got us already."

A black and white blob slid down *Liberty*'s hull.

"I'm not cleaning that," Dave said. "I'm scared of heights."

Chuck left the spaceport and drove through the city streets at a low hover. Here, vehicles still travelled exclusively along the blacktop. There were no skyways, because airborne traffic disrupted the flight paths of the giant birds, which were a protected species. So Jimmy had to sit back and accept their slow progress along the narrow side streets Chuck insisted were shortcuts. They passed several groups of children playing ball games on the road, which slowed them down even more, but they eventually arrived at the antique shop.

Jimmy jumped out of the car as Chuck slowed to a stop. He rushed to the door, backpack slung over one shoulder. "Aww, no!"

"What is it?" Dave called.

"The door's locked." He aimed his digipad at a sign on the door, translating the message. "Says he's gone to lunch."

Chuck frowned at the late afternoon hour on his watch, then shrugged. "I guess we'll have to wait. Good thing it's still a nice day."

Queue thunder.

"What do storm clouds look like here?" Dave asked.

"I'm guessing those big dark ones rolling in from behind us," Chuck answered as he checked his rear vision mirror. "Hey, Jimbo! Better get in here or you'll get zapped into an Irish crisp!"

Jimmy legged it back to the car and threw himself in as the first raindrops fell.

"I left Ireland because of the rain," Jimmy complained. "Now I have to sit in it again."

Eddie chuckled. "You left Ireland and moved to London to escape rain? Smart move. Rain is rain. You can't stop it. The shopkeeper will be back soon, and then we'll be inside."

So they sat there in the relative comfort of Chuck's Vogel. He refused to play any music, because the guys always made fun of his interest in jazz. The rain pelted so hard that it would have been difficult to hear music anyway. It covered the windscreen with such heavy streaks of water that it was almost impossible to see through. Jimmy likened it to being blind drunk.

A rumbling thunder took them by surprise and all four men tensed, then laughed at each other. Then the car shook, as if the hand of God himself had grabbed the vehicle. Chuck gingerly pulled back the sunroof slider. One of the gigantic birds sat on his roof, staring at the lawyer. Bird and man faced off for a few seconds before Chuck closed the slider.

"There's a bird on my roof," he said.

"Not good for the paint," Eddie noted.

"No," Chuck said. He looked in the rear vision mirror to see Dave and Jimmy nodding. Behind them, a white sludge ran down the car's rear window. "It just pooped on my car."

Eddie twisted around to have a look. "Hmm. Good thing it's raining, eh?"

Chuck said no more after that. He kept his cars meticulously washed and polished, and the thought of giant bird droppings on his Vogel made him sick. One hour passed, then a second, then a third. Another bird landed on the Vogel's bonnet and had a good old natter to the bird on the roof. Then the rain softened to a shower and the two birds finally left. To Chuck, the sound of their claws scratching the paintwork as they took off sent a shiver down his spine.

The shopkeeper was still a no-show. Jimmy tapped impatiently on the box. He was about to call it quits when two men wearing dark coats left the shop. They kept their collars high, hats close to their brow, and their heads low.

"They're like something out of an old gangster movie," Chuck said.

"I don't like the look of this," Eddie said. He turned to face Dave and Jimmy in the back. "Did that shopkeeper seem legit to you?"

Dave shrugged. "Sure. He was just a little old guy."

"Maybe he owes money," Jimmy suggested.

"To humans?" Chuck asked. "How many humans have you seen in this city besides us? This is weird."

The two suspicious men climbed into a car across the road, did a U-turn, and drove away. When they were out of sight, Eddie took off his seatbelt.

"I'm going to check it out," he said. "You guys stay here."

"You don't want backup?" Chuck asked.

"I used to roll with unsavoury types," Eddie said. "I'll be fine."

Eddie stepped out onto the wet footpath and moved casually towards the shop. A post-storm shower lingered, but it was nothing like the recent downpour. Eddie cupped his hands around his eyes and peered through the shop window. Then he tried the door and it opened. The other guys waited silently in the car.

Eddie reappeared and waved them over. They hurried to the shop. Eddie had left the curtain closed, and they soon learned why. The place was an absolute mess. Furniture lay splintered and strewn about. Bookcases were toppled, their contents spread on the floor like the blood of a murder victim. Every cupboard door was open, contents emptied. Rugs, some of them torn to shreds, were piled on top of couches or against the walls.

"What the hell happened here?" Jimmy asked.

"Are they gone?" came a muffled voice.

"Who?" Dave asked into thin air.

"The thugs."

"Yeah, they drove off," Dave answered.

A wall panel opened. Several tentacled eyes peered out in multiple directions before the old shopkeeper emerged. He looked frazzled.

"Are you okay?" Eddie asked. "Did they hurt you?"

The shopkeeper mumbled something in his native tongue before answering in English. "I'm fine. Those thugs were looking for something. They locked the front door, closed the curtains, and yelled at me. Then they started destroying the place."

"What were they looking for?" Chuck asked.

"I don't know. They kept saying, 'The orb! The orb! Where's the orb?' I said I didn't know what an orb was. I've never even heard the word. They said they'd kill me if they didn't find it. I got scared and hid in this secret wall when they were tearing up another room." He laughed. "This is an old building. It once housed a counterrevolutionary cell during the last dictatorship. Plenty of places to hide stuff, including people." Then he looked more closely at Dave and Jimmy. "Oh, I know you two."

"Yes, I bought this box," Jimmy said. He pulled it out of his backpack

The shopkeeper's eyes blinked one after the other and his mouth dropped. "The box! They wanted the box!"

"What?" Chuck asked. "That waste of two hundred EsCes?"

"I should have charged you a hundred times more than that." The shopkeeper marched up to Jimmy and puffed out his belly into Jimmy's crotch. Tentacle eyes stretched up to Jimmy's face. "They ruined my shop because of that box. They wanted to kill me."

Jimmy drummed his fingers nervously against the box's smooth timber. "Well, you should be happy it's not in your hands anymore."

"Damn right I'm happy. But look at this place. This was my retirement. They don't look after old people on Isthan, and especially old foreigners. What am I going to do now?"

Jimmy opened his mouth, shook his head, then frowned. "Come on, let's tally up your losses. I'll pay somehow."

The shopkeeper led him to the paystation, or what was left of it, to calculate the damages.

"Those thugs really did a number on this place, didn't they?" Dave said.

"They mean business," Eddie noted. "They even tore up the floorboards."

"You reckon we should call the police?"

Chuck, who had been inspecting some broken furniture, faced them with his arms folded. "I'd rather keep the police out of this until we leave the planet. The last thing we need is to be linked to a crime while we're trying to get investments for the resort."

"I just feel sorry for the old guy," Dave said. "What did he say they were after? An orb? What is that? A sphere or something?"

Chuck and Eddie were on their digipads before Dave finished, racing to find an answer.

"Got it," Chuck said with a grin. "You gotta be faster than that, Baldy."

"Good on ya, Nosey," Eddie taunted back.

Chuck scratched the tip of his long nose with a long middle finger. "Says here that an orb is a sphere or spherical object, or a star, or planet, or moon, or it could be an ancient term for Earth. Wow, there's more. It also has architectural, military, poetic, and photographic meanings."

"So it could be—"

"Guys!" Jimmy called. "Come here, quick!"

They rushed over. The box hummed quietly. The shop-keeper had stepped back as far as he could behind the counter. Jimmy stood rigid, unblinking.

"What's happening?" Eddie asked.

"I don't know," Jimmy said. "I was waiting for old mate to add up the damages when it started. I was tapping on its side."

Chuck stood over his shoulder. "Do it again."

"What?"

"Tap on it again."

Everyone stood back. Jimmy put one palm on the box and felt the constant thrum of energy from within. His heart raced in an odd cocktail of fear and childish wonder. He dearly wanted to know what was inside, but because he had seen too many movies, he worried that as soon as the box opened they would all be blown to smithereens, or sucked into some horrific plane of existence, or that an evil being locked away for thousands of years would be suddenly released. But because he was Jimmy, the perceived reward always outweighed the risk. He tapped his fingers on the side of the box, using the same pattern he'd improvised last time.

Click.

The guys gasped. Jimmy let go. The shopkeeper ducked. Nothing happened.

"Well that was anticlimactic," Dave said.

The box clicked again and the top half separated.

"It's opening!" Jimmy exclaimed.

Everyone stepped closer. The shopkeeper's eyes retreated into sockets all over his head. The lid opened by itself, unsupported by hinges. They stared awestruck at the object inside.

"Whoa," Jimmy said.

A brilliant blue light emanated from the box's interior, illuminating the guys' faces.

The shopkeeper opened his eyes again. "Not bad for two hundred EsCes." He pushed a bit of archaic paper with the damage bill across the counter. Jimmy was too entranced to speak or even notice the zeroes on the bill.

"You got that right," Chuck replied. He was the only one with the mental fortitude to peel his eyes away from the startling object inside the box.. He checked the price on the archaic paper. "You need to skip town. No, skip planet. Those bad guys may come back, so you need to get as far away as possible." He pulled out his digipad. "I've sent you your money. Do you like beaches?"

"Beaches?" the shopkeeper asked. "Sure. I grew up on a tropical archipelago. My people are amphibious."

"Good," Chuck continued. He wrote something down on the other side of the damage bill. "These coordinates are for a planet called Paradise. Don't worry about your belongings. Leave immediately. Go to Haven Resort and ask for Sequoia. Tell her that Chuck sent you. We are rebuilding a resort there. You can live out your retirement in or around the resort, or you can start another business. It's a quiet corner of the galaxy for now, and nobody will know where you came from. It's the least we can do for you."

The shopkeeper digested the information. Uprooting himself and disappearing among the stars was probably not how he saw his day turning out.

"Thank you," the shopkeeper said. He reached over the counter and grasped Chuck's hand with both of his. "Thank you."

"We don't even know your name," Dave said, finally disengaging himself from the box.

"I'm Kipphe Rhen."

"Do you have any dependants?" Eddie asked.

"None. I am the youngest of my sibs, and in my culture the youngest remain childless."

"That makes it easier for you to disappear. Find a disguise from some of the clothes in the shop and we'll take you to the spaceport. I'll buy you a chartered ticket to Paradise."

Kipphe repeated his thanks several times as he rounded the counter and raided the piles of clothes the thugs had left around the place.

Chuck gave Eddie his car key. "Here. Bring the car up to the door and keep it running. You can drive us back."

Eddie stared at him for all of two seconds, but in that time he realised that Chuck rarely let anyone drive his cars and that he must have been very serious about this whole situation. The lawyer in Chuck had sniffed something awry and he was taking charge of the situation. Eddie quickly got on board with Chuck's thinking and darted out of the shop.

Dave nudged Jimmy, who was still staring at the mesmerising object in his treasure box. He finally snapped out of his trance.

"We need to get out of here," Jimmy said as he closed the lid. "And we need to learn exactly what I have bought and why some bad dudes turned this place upside down looking for it."

3

AN INTROVERT'S NIGHTMARE

THE GUYS BID FAREWELL and safe passage to Kipphe at the spaceport before rushing to *Liberty* to begin their own journey. Getting away from Isthan as quickly as possible was a priority and, fortunately, it was an easy thing to do, given Isthan's rather lax interstellar travel laws. It still didn't stop Jimmy from tapping the box's same unlocking melody until it was . . . ahem . . . *drummed* into his head.

After seeing what the box contained, they were certain that they'd need a xenologist to examine it. Chuck tried to set up a meeting with an old contact on Earth, but it was proving difficult to get an appointment, mainly because his contact had died at a lovely old age some years ago.

The field of xenology was quite large, considering that it encompassed the study of every known intelligent race in the galaxy. Because of this, it was structured in two interlinked ways. The first was by race—anthropology, for example, being the xenological study of humanity (because xenology was a galactic field and humans were considered aliens to all other races). The second was by disciplines, such as xenoarchaeology, xenobiology, xenolinguistics, and so on.

Therefore, suitably qualified individuals abounded. The problem lay in finding someone within the right discipline and racial/cultural study area who could not only identify what treasure Jimmy had acquired, but who also pass on knowledge about it and maybe explain why thugs were searching for it.

Since Chuck's contacts were leading to dead ends, they resolved to go straight to Oxford and force someone to meet with them, which would hopefully generate some leads. They figured a xenoarchaeologist would do the trick. Or, if the box and its contents turned out to be not as old as originally thought, then a general xenohistorian would suffice. The first hurdle, however, was getting through Earth's customs area.

Dave hated Onishi Spaceport. The gigantic moon-based structure was the primary thoroughfare that bottle-necked all civilian traffic entering and exiting Earth. Onishi was one of—if not *the*—busiest interstellar transit points in the galaxy. To put it into context, it was an introvert's nightmare.

They were assigned an external bay on one of the myriad docking arms extending out of the massive elevator column rising from the spaceport's domed roof. Dave knew that if they weren't given an indoor hangar, then it meant Eddie was being particularly stingy with his docking fees, or the port was extremely busy and had none to spare. He sighed and gazed at Earth as *Liberty* moved into position.

Moon—yes, the moon was called Moon—happened to be passing Australia at the time, and Dave felt a surge of homesickness. He hadn't set foot on Australian soil in years. As night cast a dark shadow over the island continent, the Trans-Australian Skyway sparkled in a kinked umbrella shape. It connected all the major eastern cities from Brisbane to Hobart, then stretched west across to Perth, jutting down to include Adelaide along the way. Someone forgot to include Darwin at the far north.

The dull thud of docking clamps and the hissing of an atmospheric gangway attaching itself to *Liberty* brought Dave out of his observations. Jimmy, clutching his backpack and eager to get a move on, had already dashed for the elevator and sent himself down, so the others had to wait with interminable patience for it to come back up. They made sure to punch him in the arm when they reached him. Cameron stayed aboard to keep Eve company, though she insisted that she was "a strong, independent AI who don't need no company".

"Right, we need transport to the surface," Jimmy said as soon as the others had joined him in the docking arm.

"Hold up," Chuck said. "We need to go through customs first."

Jimmy drooped his shoulders and went to a nearby passenger cart. It beeped to life.

"Hello. Where may I take you?"

Jimmy shot a look at Chuck as he climbed aboard.

"Customs, please," Chuck told it.

"And don't spare the horses," Jimmy added.

"There are no horses permitted anywhere outside the Aaliyah Abbas Cargo Terminal. Please dock at the cargo terminal to declare your equine cargo."

"We don't have any horses," Eddie said. "It was just a turn of phrase."

"Very well," the cart's AI said. "To customs!"

After a jolt of minor whiplash, the guys were zooming down the central lane of the docking arm, passing countless bays of incoming and outgoing passengers. The number of passenger carts increased the closer they came to the elevators. Before they reached the elevators, the passenger traffic became so thick that Jimmy had opted to leave the cart and walk the rest of the way. The others quickly followed. Dave offered a word of thanks to the cart AI and left it stuck in the hectic indoor traffic jam.

The elevators were arranged around a central column higher than the spaceport's width. At least twenty docking arms converged on this floor and there were people moving in every direction. Jimmy pushed and squeezed his way to an elevator only to find it filled with travellers. Many people, both human and alien, wore colourful sports jerseys and carried footballs—*real* footballs of the black and white chequered kind. One group in red and white cheered not far away.

"Whose bright idea was it to come to Earth during the AFI Galactic Cup?" Eddie asked.

"How was I supposed to know?" Chuck asked defensively. "You wanted a meeting with a xenologist. The best are on Earth." Someone shouldered him as an elevator opened. "Look at this yobbo," he muttered.

"Yes, I forgot you don't follow any sports," Eddie said.

No sooner had an elevator arrived and disgorged its occupants than a new set of highly-strung travellers piled in.

"This is madness," Dave said. He was feeling supremely uncomfortable with all the noise and commotion.

"Chuck," Jimmy said, "you're the tallest. Look over everyone's heads and see where the next elevator is coming."

Chuck stood on his toes for added height. "There. Follow me." He grabbed Jimmy's hand, but Jimmy smacked it away. "Sorry," Chuck said. "That was an ex-wife déjà vu moment."

They marched through the crowd like a snowplough. Chuck used his most authoritative lawyer voice to move people before he reached them. They managed to reach the front of a group standing by a cluster of elevator doors. One football fan with bright blue frizzy hair was about to complain, but Dave folded his arms. The stretched threads on his shirt sleeves ensured the man's silence.

The elevator opened and a torrent of suited people charged into the throng of football fans. Jimmy surged forth and claimed the elevator but was quickly pushed against its back wall as everyone else crammed in. People mercifully jabbed at buttons and the doors closed. Jimmy felt the shape of the alien box against his back, Dave had a football fan's gigantic belly prodding him, Chuck was assaulted by a redheaded woman's ponytail, and Eddie had some weird little girl staring up at him.

"Looks like we have more Sattalo fans than human fans in here," one of the aliens said. They were dressed and groomed in the red and white garb of their home team.

"Don't matter how many Sattalo fans are here," said the large man in front of Dave. "Won't make your team play any better. You're on our home turf. This year's cup belongs to Earth."

"The only way Earth will win is if someone is bribed, which sounds about right," someone else chimed in.

Aaaaand there it is, Dave thought. The rivalry began even before the fans made it planetside.

"Let's not start anything," Chuck warned, looking down on everyone. "Wouldn't want to be turned back for disorderly conduct and not see Earth lose, would we?"

The few Earth supporters stared at Chuck, gobsmacked that a human could even suggest that their team would lose. The Sattalos laughed, and the laughter carried them through to the end of the elevator ride.

The terminal was even busier than the docking arm, but Onishi administrators had been wise enough to keep a few lanes free for non-AFI visitors. It was a short wait before the guys checked in their only item. At a robot assistant's behest, Jimmy put his backpack through the luggage scanner. The scanner monitor showed a dark square inside the bag and it was enough to arouse suspicion. The robot assistant signalled for a human supervisor to help.

The human approached. Her name tag read SHERYN ARENAS, and she carried herself with the surety of someone who had discovered a plethora of prohibited items over the years. "Please come with me, sirs." She picked up the backpack and directed them to a table out of the way of the main processing area.

Jimmy tried to soften her. "So, Arenas? You don't look like an Arenas."

She plonked the bag onto a table and regarded him with a blank stare that mocked the stupidity of his statement. "What does an Arenas look like?"

Jimmy gulped. "Tanned?"

She rolled her eyes. "Before I open this bag, can you please tell me about its contents?"

"It's a——" Jimmy started.

"It's a solid cube of finished timber from a rare alien tree," Chuck said. "We are getting it valued."

Jimmy realised that was a smart thing to say and let the lawyer do the talking.

The supervisor's face remained neutral as she unzipped the backpack, peeling front and back open like a banana and staring at the box for a moment. She slipped her hands into a pair of disposable gloves and handled the box like a museum director.

Not unlike a xenologist, Chuck thought.

"What material is it?" the supervisor asked.

"Wood."

"I mean what species?"

"Oh, we don't know exactly. We were hoping a specialist could identify it and help with the valuation. But we do know it is alien."

"And very old," Dave added.

She turned it in her hands, studying it closely. "How do you know it's alien? Where did you find it? I don't mean to be rude, but it's my job to ask."

"Well, at least you're not a Karen," Chuck said and finished it with a dad-laugh.

Sheryn-Not-Karen smiled thinly. Chuck had never been questioned so thoroughly by a customs officer. Back in his heyday, if he had been on a work trip, he would have harangued her with a long list of laws and regulations about privacy and customer service until she saw sense and let him through. But this situation was more delicate.

"We found it in an antique shop," he answered. "We were told it was of non-human origin, but I think my friend here got gypped."

The supervisor set the box down on the table and started tapping on it while jotting something on a digipad. Jimmy drew a light breath and watched her hand, hoping that she wouldn't inadvertently tap the code to unlock it.

"I have cleared this article through customs," Sheryn Arenas, Onishi Spaceport Customs Supervisor Extraordinaire, said. "The scanners show that it is a solid block of wood, as you say." She stuffed the box back in the bag and zipped it shut. "I hope the valuation goes well. Please enjoy your stay on Earth."

She gestured with a hand in the general direction of the planet, which was code for "Get lost". Jimmy slung the bag on his back and took long strides towards a shuttle terminal, partly because he was itching to get to the university, but also because he could feel the supervisor's hot stare boring into the back of his head. The others hurried after him, for they had a professor to speak to, and no time to lose.

4

THE PROFESSOR

THE SHUTTLE TOOK THEM to Heathrow Airport, which was just a mini Onishi, only with more British people. This made it only slightly more bearable for Dave. Since Heathrow was London's largest international airport, it also handled shuttle traffic to and from Moon. Being the UK's only entry and exit point for interplanetary travel, this meant there were millions more travellers within its terminals. To cater for the comings and goings of these highly-strung passengers, Heathrow had expanded northwards to the M4 motorway, claiming the land of the old villages of Harmondsworth, Sipson, and Harlington. Of course, if one had a personal spacecraft and somewhere to park it on Earth, they could bypass Heathrow altogether. Unfortunately, Eddie sold his home outside of London where *Liberty* was built, so they could not return there. Dave and Jimmy were apartment renters at the time they skipped off on their first voyage on *Liberty*, and the only properties Chuck's ex-wife had left him in the entire British Isles were not large enough to land an oversized flying watermelon, so now they had to manage with public transport.

Heathrow was busier than normal due to the British football fans waiting for flights to Paris for the AFI Galactic Cup. Dave's nerves were disappearing faster than the fuse to a stick of dynamite. Soon, he would be at the end of his tether, and it was never safe when an eighty-kilogram introverted bodybuilding accountant loses his cool. In fact, he nearly reached that point as Chuck and Eddie argued over the fastest means to get to Oxford. In the end, they opted for a skybus.

The UK had a well-planned system of skyways above London's urban sprawl, and their bus took a roughly easterly route to Oxford. The two cities had expanded towards each other—London, because it was London and people kept moving in, and Oxford because of its galactic importance as a centre for higher learning, particularly xenological studies. The skybus reached London's eastern extremity, which bordered the protected belt of greenery aptly known as the Chilterns Area of Outstanding Natural Beauty. Butting against the other side of this scenic landscape was Oxford.

Chuck pointed to the university. At their vantage point, they could see the centuries-old buildings that memorialised its illustrious history. But to the north, the university had gobbled up a narrow stretch of fields when it built its new Xenology Department and established the first Galactic Institute of Xenology. This boom in academic activity resulted in several new colleges, dormitories, museums, and research buildings on university land, as well as the expansion of the city itself to accommodate the growing interest in everything alien.

Because Chuck had some experience with the department, he briefly described its history. His intellectual tone and almost documentary-style storytelling even had other skybus passengers hanging onto every word. Chuck wrapped up his history lesson as the skybus landed at a large intercity terminal.

"Which way?" Jimmy asked when they had alighted. He was itching to move.

While looking at Jimmy, Chuck pointed in the general direction of where they needed to go. Jimmy started power walking.

"Don't you want a taxi?" Eddie called after him.

"It'll take too long. Follow me."

They hailed a taxi five minutes later, and three minutes after that they arrived at the xenology administration building at Oxford University. The receptionist was human and quite cheerful.

"What can I do for you gentlemen today?"

Jimmy dumped his bag on the reception desk and took out the box. "We need a xenologist to inspect this and tell us what it is."

The receptionist regarded Jimmy as if he didn't need a xenologist to tell him that a wooden cube was a wooden cube.

"Um, sure. We have a great many xenologists here, covering all the specialities of the field. Do you have an idea of what it might be, so I can help you choose the right one?"

"Well," Jimmy started, "it's an object."

"What does it do?"

"Shines blue."

"You mean there's something in there?"

Jimmy looked at his friends for approval. Dave and Eddie were frozen in place, unsure how much information should be doled out. Chuck gave the go-ahead. They were, after all, in the right place for it. Jimmy tapped on the box and opened the lid a bit wider than a crack.

A blue radiance caught the receptionist's eyes. He looked at Jimmy and smiled. "Professor Jurjik Sowenso. Fourth floor. Room 410." He checked his computer. "The professor has no appointments right now. I will tell him you are on your way."

Jimmy snapped the box shut, bagged it, and hurriedly thanked the receptionist before moving on, friends in tow. Up a few floors, along some corridors, an about-face after going in the wrong direction, and finally they were in the right place. They rounded a corner and saw a pudgy green alien in a dark green-brown tweed suit.

"Professor Sowenso, I presume?" Chuck asked.

The alien jumped backwards and darted into a nearby office, slamming the door shut.

"Not the greeting I anticipated," Dave said.

A gold plaque on the office door read: PROFESSOR J. SOWENSO, XENOARCHAEOLOGY. Jimmy knocked and politely asked to be admitted, but silence answered.

"Professor Sowenso, didn't Reception tell you we were coming?" Jimmy asked.

"Go away!"

The guys looked at each other, confused. Surely this eminent scholar wanted to see the secrets of Jimmy's wooden box.

"Dave," Jimmy said. "You think you can put your muscles to good use?"

"That's not what they're for," Dave replied. Whether he was aware or not, his biceps flexed, almost as if they were agreeing with him and were ready to argue the point.

"Come on, we've made it this far."

"Coast is clear," Eddie said.

Dave scanned the hallway, making sure they were not being watched. Thankfully, the building designers had opted for an older style and used hinged doors. Dave slammed the door with a muscular arm. The heavy timber withstood the barrage, but he tried a few more times. Then Eddie leaned in and opened the door towards them.

"It's on backwards," Eddie said. "And unlocked."

They filed in.

"Seems you forgot to lock the door, Professor," Jimmy said. He scanned the room. "Now where is he?"

The office was small and cold, with a meagre window overlooking a grassy quadrangle. An executive desk dominated the middle of the room, but books—actual books—were piled high on either side of a computer monitor and an open digipad. More books and artefacts lined the walls. Dave drooled over them.

"Maybe he jumped out the window," Eddie suggested.

"This sucks," Jimmy said. He sat on a stool in a huff. The stool grunted and Jimmy jumped off in a hurry. Then the stool reformed into Sowenso.

"You're a shapeshifter?" Dave asked.

"Very observant," Sowenso grumbled. He rubbed his back. "I'm going to feel that for weeks. Why can't you people leave me alone? Who are you, anyway?"

"Reception said we could speak with you," Chuck explained. He introduced himself and his friends.

Sowenso sat at his desk with a sigh. He rubbed his green cheeks. "Why are you here bothering me in between classes?"

"Professor, we have something to show you," Jimmy said. "Didn't Reception tell you?"

"Reception told me nothing."

"Hmm." Jimmy produced the wooden box and placed it on the only uncluttered spot on Sowenso's desk.

Sowenso regarded it cautiously. "No . . . Could it be?"

"You know what it is?" Jimmy asked. He drew closer to the desk.

"It looks like an orb carrier. Have you opened it?"

Jimmy nodded.

"And there *is* an orb inside?"

Jimmy nodded again.

Sowenso slumped. "So you're not here to *find* an orb. You're here to learn about an orb you've already *found*."

All four men nodded.

"You have no idea what this is, do you?"

Two of them shook their heads; the other two nodded.

"So you do know what it is?" Sowenso asked Dave and Chuck, who had nodded.

"No, we don't," Dave said.

"But you nodded!"

Jimmy groaned. "Will you help us?"

Sowenso stared. He rubbed his cheeks again before furiously shaking his hands. "All right, fine! Let's open it. No, wait! Close the curtains first. And lock the door."

They did as he said. Sowenso tapped the unlocking code and the box separated. A brilliant blue ball, smooth as glass and with a swirling iridescent centre, hovered in front of his face.

"By Senther's eye," Sowenso swore, "it *is* an orb! You have the Blue Orb of Princess Dakay!" He reached out to touch it but thought better of it and retracted his hand.

"Princess Dakay?" Jimmy asked.

Sowenso shook the sense back into himself. "There were seven orbs built by the last king of Hajar and given to each of his children. Princess Dakay was supposedly one of them. We don't have many records of the ancient Hajari Kingdom, but what we do know is that these orbs were symbols of power and authority." He tapped on his datapad until he found what he needed. "See here."

He showed them a photo of an ancient artwork masterfully carved and coloured on a stone wall. It depicted a throne with an elderly alien king and seven younger people arrayed before him, each holding an orb of a different colour.

"This one here is Princess Dakay," Sowenso explained, pointing to one of the females, "and that is Prince Barshun holding the red orb. We don't know who the others are, but we are certain they are siblings. Of the few texts we have found and translated, all mention the orbs as being gifts to the king's children. Only two orbs are on record as being found." He gazed at his human visitors. "You have the third."

Jimmy's jaw dropped. Dave reached over and closed it for him.

Chuck cleared his throat and paced the small room. "So, one of seven orbs from a dead kingdom. Any money in them?"

Sowenso scoffed. "Of course there is money. You won't get any from Oxford, though. In fact, Oxford sold its green and purple orbs to a collector and xenoarchaeologist by the name of Count Karl Friedrich von Mein. If it's money you want, he's your buyer. Oh, you haven't told anyone else about the orb, have you?"

"No," Jimmy replied.

"Good, because once Mein finds out you have one, he won't stop pestering you until you sell it to him. Although he probably has this place monitored, so he will find out sooner or later."

"What are they worth?" Jimmy asked.

"He bought the green and purple orbs together for five million EsCes."

"Oh, *really*?" Jimmy put his hands on his hips and faced Chuck with a smug expression. "Not bad for two hundred, is it?"

Chuck crossed the room and shook Jimmy's hand. "Well done," he mumbled. "I'm sorry I doubted you."

Sowenso sighed heavily and pushed himself away from the desk. He went to the window and peered between the curtains. "What do you plan to do with the orb?"

Jimmy glanced at his friends. "I don't know yet."

"We do need money for the resort," Chuck said.

With the recent string of unlucky investment meetings, their resort was in dire need of funding. While two-and-a-half million EsCes for one orb wasn't enough to cover the costs of such a grand project, it was better than nothing. "Do you want to buy it?"

Sowenso looked at his feet and then spun around. "No . . . yes . . . no. No, I don't. I do, but I don't."

"Well, why?" Dave asked. "Or why not? Or . . . what?"

The professor sighed and rubbed his cheeks more furiously than ever before. "Count Mein is now the galaxy's preeminent

Hajari researcher. He used his vast wealth to buy access to and control of artefacts, dig sites, and previously published research to further his own academic goals. And he has a private security team to protect his interests. I was once one of a handful of Hajari experts, but none of us are allowed near the subject anymore."

"Sounds like we should avoid him," Chuck said.

"Yes," Sowenso said. "Avoid him like the Great Plague of 2120. There is something greatly unnerving about the man."

A collective sigh filled the room.

Now, for anyone who had known Jimmy for a respectable length of time, they would have noticed some tell-tale signs creep onto his face at that moment. With eyelids squinted and his head tilting slightly upwards, his eyes began to dart in all directions in minuscule movements. He was thinking, imagining, planning.

"I say we research it ourselves," Jimmy said.

"What about Count Mein?" Dave asked.

"What's the worst that could happen? Has he ever killed anyone?"

"He will slap you on the wrist and tell you to stop," Sowenso said. "I think because you are clearly amateurs, he might find the whole situation amusing and let you off lightly. If he knows you have the orb, he will try to buy it from you."

Jimmy thought pensively. "Okay, so it's not like he's killed anyone before."

Sowenso shrugged. "One historian went missing some years ago. A colleague and close friend of mine named Doctor Shay Shahidi. He was . . . rather insistent on continuing his research."

"We've dealt with shady people before," Eddie said. He elbowed Dave in the ribs. "Haven't we?"

"Don't remind me." The memory of the gang boss Harlequin Grover who had wanted to bed him and kill him at the same time was still raw.

The elderly professor shuffled back to his desk. "You know, Mein keeps a tight grip on Hajari research. But I think you four can slip under his radar." He motioned for them to come closer. They did so. "You haven't shown the orb to anyone?"

"The antique shop owner where I bought it," Jimmy told him.

"And the receptionist downstairs," Chuck said.

Sowenso paled. "Oh, dear. I think your identities are already blown. If Mein is keeping tabs on the department, the receptionists would most certainly report to him."

He scanned his bookshelves as if there might be listening devices or cameras, then returned the orb to its box.

"You must leave as soon as possible and get out of the star system," he went on softly. "Learn all you can about the blue orb. Find its homeworld. The orb lived with the offspring of a king—think of the wealth that might have surrounded it! No archaeologist has managed to find an orb's homeworld, let alone the capital planet of the Hajari Kingdom. If you manage to do this, who knows what riches you'll uncover? With that wealth and fame, we can knock Mein off his perch and Oxford can regain control of Hajari research."

Jimmy was just about shaking with excitement. "Just tell us what we need to do."

Sowenso spoke even more quietly. "I've heard a rumour that Mein is excavating a Hajari site on a planet called

Akalam. I'll give you the coordinates. You need to go there and get some leads. It's risky, but I have nowhere else to send you."

"Right into the belly of the beast," Eddie said. "Should be fun. What sort of information should we gather?"

"You need leads. Locations of dig sites, records of Hajari texts and artefacts—don't worry, I'll give you a copy of my secret hoard of Hajari materials."

Sowenso started navigating his computer. He spoke as he clicked through folders. "Don't let him win. He's a bully, and I don't trust his intentions. If he secures all seven orbs, who knows what immense wealth he might accumulate and what he would do with it? Historical inquiry isn't about money. It's about knowledge and understanding. But Count Mein is poisoning my profession, and I am powerless to stop him."

"We'll stop him!" Jimmy said. "You can count on . . . uh, no, not *count*. You can *depend* on us!"

"Whoa, wait a minute," Dave said, hands up. "Let's think about this."

"What's there to think about?" Jimmy asked. "We have an orb, the other guy has three. He won't know we're coming for him, and—" he faced Sowenso "—let's be honest, I like the idea of claiming a few ancient treasures for myself."

Sowenso waved at him. "I'll forgive you for that. Consider it your payment."

"But we're not archaeologists," Dave retorted. "This is way over our heads."

"But we have four heads," Jimmy replied. He looked to Chuck for support, since Chuck was the undisputed master of debates.

Chuck scratched his chin. "He makes a good argument."

"And Eddie," Jimmy continued, "we'll need your ship to travel the stars and gather said treasures."

"Christie and the kids won't be happy about it," Eddie warned.

"Oh, come on," Jimmy said. "They're living on a gorgeous garden world surrounded by lovely tree people. And they have my mother for company."

"Your mother is a pain in the neck," Eddie said, and Dave nodded in agreement. "But I'll tag along. This reeks of adventure, and I'd hate to leave it all to you guys. Maybe I can find some Hajari jewellery for Christie as a 'thank you' gift. Here, Professor, give us all the data you think we'll need." He dropped his digipad on Sowenso's desk.

Jimmy jumped for joy. "Great!" He turned back to Dave. "How about it? You're the odd one out now."

Dave wrinkled his nose in thought, making eye contact with Sowenso. "Did the Hajari write books?"

Sowenso nodded. "Plenty of them."

"Would they still exist?"

"Of course. They used a hardy material. I had several volumes, but Count Mein took them all. If you find an intact Hajari site, there should be books there."

"May I take some?" Dave raised his eyebrows hopefully.

"I don't see why not," Sowenso replied. "As long as you let me read them. In fact, to hell with Mein, grab some for me too!"

Dave whipped back to Jimmy. "I'm in."

Jimmy shook hands with his friends. "This will be fun." He collected the orb vessel and zipped it safely in his backpack.

"Sounds like we have a lot of work on our plates, lads," Eddie said. "Don't worry, Professor, we'll stop Mein and find the other orbs."

Sowenso stood and reached over his desk, clasping each man's hands in turn. "You are good people. Make sure you don't die out there. Xenoarchaeology is dangerous work, German noblemen or not. When you leave, tell the receptionist you couldn't find me. He knows I am a shapeshifter. That should hopefully keep Count Mein's ire off my back. I can't say the same for you, though. Be careful."

The guys thanked Sowenso for his help and left his office in good spirits. Thus began a new adventure for our four intrepid friends. They were truly above their heads, as Dave noted, but cocksure enough not to care about it. They just had to leave Earth as quickly as possible.

5

ESCAPING EARTH

THEY RUSHED THE TAXI driver, then they rushed the skybus driver. At Heathrow, among the throng of businesspeople, travelling families, and Paris-bound football fans, rushing was the name of the game. But such a large volume of people rushed rather slowly, thanks to the strict British check-in protocols. Eventually, they made it to a shuttle bound for Moon.

The shuttle roared and boomed as it flew upwards into space. The noise of its engines dropped off considerably once the starry sky showed, but the noise of its passengers did not.

Dave's tether began to shorten again, and he checked his watch every few seconds. It was a twelve-minute trip to Moon today. To keep his mind occupied, he complained inwardly about how silly and uncreative it was to name Earth's moon *Moon*. He spent the rest of the time thinking of better names, trying desperately to ignore the kids kicking the back of his chair and the three babies screaming like opera singers.

Chuck, the sixty-year-old forty-year-old, kept his eyes closed and pinched the bridge of his nose. Jimmy seemed oblivious to the whole thing and was even trying to make conversation with Chuck, who simply nodded or shook his head in reply. Eddie, on the other hand, had lapsed into old habits. He scanned the shuttle cabin, eyeing everyone. He tapped Dave and motioned him to lean forwards, then put his head between Chuck's and Jimmy's in the seats in front.

"I think we are being followed," Eddie said. "Two guys a few rows back. They won't stop staring at us. Don't look at them."

Jimmy looked at them. "They look like office drones."

"One way to blend in, I suppose," Dave said. He had been an office drone in a previous life before he went on a holiday and never returned.

They worked out a plan of how to escape their followers, if they really were being followed. Once they reached the spaceport, they would leg it to *Liberty*. It wasn't the best plan, but they liked their chances.

"Approaching Onishi Civilian Spaceport," the pilot said.

The flight attendant went through the routine docking spiel with the passengers. Mercifully, the passengers' chatter quietened to an acceptable level as they listened. Dave had his hand on his seatbelt, ready to unlatch the moment the flight attendant said they could leave. Eddie's was already undone. He had the aisle seat and had silently acknowledged his role to block the aisle so his friends could make a quick escape.

The pilot glided into a shuttle hangar and landed in an empty. The flight attendant thanked everyone for using the shuttle service and opened the door.

Madness ensued. Businesspeople were suddenly terribly late for meetings. They jumped out of their seats and crowded into the aisle. Children, who had enjoyed the shuttle trip immensely, now couldn't wait to get off.

Eddie stood in the aisle and a line of grumpy passengers stretched behind him. Dave got out and took point, then Jimmy and Chuck left their seats. Eddie felt people pushing him from behind. Now that his friends were moving, he also moved, but he couldn't help but look around to see the faces of those he had stalled.

One of the suspicious dudes stared back at him. He was about Eddie's height, had a thick crop of jet-black hair, and wore a mix of black and dark grey casual business attire.

When thinking back on this moment, Eddie still cannot fathom why he said what he said, what brashness had motivated him to blurt out the most direct question he had asked since proposing to his wife. "Are you following us?"

And, with unsmiling straightforwardness, the other man, whom Eddie decided to call Jet, inadvertently said, "Yes."

Eddie's eyes went wide, and his arms acted before his brain could think. He pushed the man with all his might. The fellow toppled backwards into the arms of his colleague, but the forcefulness of it created a domino effect. Passengers dropped one after the other. Eddie didn't watch to see if they made it all the way to the rear of the aisle.

"Run!" he called out to his friends, bolting after them. He muttered an apology as he passed the flight attendant and jumped down all the exit stairs in one leap. If his brain had worked faster, he would have told the flight attendant to stall the goons.

Dave was nearly at the exit door already, with Jimmy was not far behind, despite carrying the bulky backpack.

"What happened?" Chuck asked as Eddie caught up.

"They were following us," Eddie told him.

"We half-expected that already."

"I asked them."

"You asked them?"

"Yeah."

They made it to the door, entered together and kept going to the departures terminal to find it busier than expected.

"*Bloody Hell*," Jimmy said. A large, scary poster advertising *Bloody Hell*, a horror film, dangled from the ceiling, catching his attention.

"No time for that," Chuck said, snapping Jimmy out of movie madness.

They queued for a security check, passed it, and kept going.

"We've been spotted," Dave said.

Everyone looked and saw both bad guys standing at the security section. One of them pointed. It was Jet, and he most certainly had a beef with Eddie.

"Let's move, guys," Eddie said.

"We need to get to the central column," Chuck said. "Onwards!"

They charged headlong into a crowd of incoming football fans, pushing them aside. The fans, all Canadians, and apparently lost in the departures terminal, apologised for being in the way. They parted, giving the guys a clear view of an AI cart rank.

"Hello," a cart said. "Where may I take you?"

"To the elevators," Jimmy said. "And please hurry. We are being followed."

The cart skidded on the polished floor and the AI sounded its horn, clearing a path. The shrill noise went straight to Dave's head. He sat on the back seat, facing the rear, and saw their pursuers commandeer a cart already in use, despite there being over a dozen free ones not ten metres away.

What followed was a "hot pursuit" that averaged fifteen kilometres per hour, weaving through crowds and solid objects. Count Mein's goons were gaining on them.

"Use your tree-trunk legs to batter them away," Jimmy told Dave.

Better my tree-trunk legs than your chicken legs, Dave thought. He kicked out, but the other cart was too far away. Seeing the defence tactic, the goons assaulted from the flank. They bossed their cart AI to move alongside the guys and started reaching for Jimmy's backpack. Jimmy, seeing this, acted instantly with a terrific right hook against the one with the darkest hair he'd ever seen. The fellow dropped off the other side and the cart stopped so his pal could pick him up.

"Ow," Jimmy said, shaking his hand. "That was the hardest jaw I've ever felt, and I've hit more than a few."

The cart turned a corner, screeching loudly on the polished floor. Couple that with the shouts of irate passengers, Jimmy yelling obscenities, and the near-incoherent spaceport announcements over the public address system, and Dave was nearly ready to explode. They skidded to a stop by the elevators. Hopefully this madness would be over soon.

"Don't suppose you could crash into that other cart for us?" Jimmy asked the AI.

"I will block them." It sped away and parked itself across the middle of the large corridor.

Chuck grunted, clearly unimpressed, but there was not much else to do. They scoured the circle of elevators until they found one approaching their level. The crowd around them pressed closer in anticipation.

Someone rough-handled Dave's arm and spun him around. "Hey, we need to talk to you four."

It was Jet. At that point, Dave's world froze. He heard nothing, felt nothing, and certainly thought nothing of the well-dressed thug as he picked him up off the floor and hurled him into Thug Number 2. By the time the elevator doors opened, everyone was too stunned to step in, so the guys had it all to themselves.

"You flattened him, mate!" Jimmy said. He put a hand on Dave's shoulder and laughed.

"Ahhhhh!" Dave shouted. "No more touching, no more yelling. Let's just get out of here."

"Right," Chuck said. "Easy, big fella. We're nearly there."

Dave, suffering sensory overload and itching to leave, was the first to exit the elevator and barrel through the startled passengers wishing to get on. He barked demands to move out of the way, which they did, because, unbeknown to him, he had torn his shirt when he attacked Count Mein's thug, and now he looked like a pro wrestler striding up to the ring for a fight.

They arrived at *Liberty*'s airlock without further incident. Eddie went straight to the cockpit and set a course for Akalam using the coordinates supplied by Professor Sowenso.

"Oh, Dave," Eve said, "you look like you've been mugged."

Cameron zoomed into the galley. "Master Dave! What happened?"

Eddie answered for him. "We got jumped by some bad dudes."

"Why?" Eve and Cameron said in unison.

"Because Jimmy's blue ball happens to be extremely rare, and now we are amateur archaeologists bent on learning more about it."

They all went to the cockpit.

"Not just that," Jimmy said as he plonked himself into a chair. "There's treasure to be found, and we're going to find it."

Dave sat and tilted his head back, kissing his hermit dreams goodbye as Eddie powered up *Liberty*'s engine.

Next stop: Akalam.

♥♣♦♠

"They got away from us," said the breathless voice through the audiolink.

"It is not like you to fail," came the measured reply. When there was silence on the line, the voice continued. "Good, you say nothing because there is nothing to say. No excuse. We have lost them for now, but they will re-surface again."

"Thank you, my lord."

"Send your surveillance photos. I will alert the organisation. They won't step one foot in our territory without us knowing about it."

"And then we pounce."

"No, we are not cats. Cats are creeps. We do not pounce. I am still deciding what we should do with these four troublemakers." A pause. "Come to me. I have an idea."

6

ANUS OF THE GALAXY, THY NAME IS AKALAM

I<small>F THE GALAXY HAD</small> an anus, it would be Akalam. This dark, unforgiving place sat in a corner of the galaxy where few people travelled, rightly out of sight and out of mind. *Liberty* approached the ringed planet and the guys studied it from the cockpit. Its charcoal surface was crisscrossed with white-yellow fissures and dotted with glowing volcanoes and orange seas.

"This place stinks," Eve said.

"You're telling me," Eddie replied.

"No, I mean it really stinks. The atmosphere is highly sulphuric. You will most certainly need an enviro suit."

"Huh," Eddie said. "Understood. Are we ready to land? Where *do* we land?"

They circled the planet. A few ships were detected travelling along the same route to and from the planet's ring. They may have been mining vessels. No space stations orbited the planet, but Eve did detect a lone radio signal from the surface. It could have been an end-point for the mining vessels.

"Must be the dig site," Chuck said.

Eddie followed the signal. On the way, a larger, more rect-angular vessel exited the atmosphere and rocketed towards them. The guys tensed. Eve noted that it was flying on the same line as the others they saw—and the same shape too—so it was probably safe to ignore it. On the 3D display, as the two ships passed, they looked like wooden blocks that a toddler would pick up and slip through holes of matching shapes.

Jimmy tapped Eddie on the shoulder. "You know what I've been thinking? We should install some autocannons on this ship. The galaxy is a dangerous place."

"Where am I going to get cannons from?" Eddie asked. "Do you really want this ship to get impounded at every spaceport?"

"Just a suggestion."

"I wouldn't mind some autocannons," Eve whispered.

"You're not getting autocannons!" Eddie told her.

The land below started to take on a more recognisable shape. It was very clear now that the surface was utterly destroyed. In the far distance, a lava lake bubbled below a towering volcano. The volcano spewed forth ash clouds lanced with lightning strikes. Big cracks in the ground suggested terrible earthquakes.

"These Hajari must have been lava surfers or something," Jimmy said. "Can you imagine living here?"

"I cannot see any reason to live here," Dave said.

And yet, that is exactly what a small group of people were doing. Below them, quite possibly carved out of pumice, was a large and deep archaeological dig site. Building foundations and roadways had been uncovered, and who knew what else. Not far from the site was a modern settlement. It looked bigger than an encampment, but not so permanent or established as to be a village.

"I'm setting her down here," Eddie said, choosing a spot near some other ships.

"It is terribly hot here," Eve said as Eddie touched down. "Can you cool-weather Brits handle it?"

Jimmy jumped out of his seat and left the cockpit. The others followed. "Got no choice. I'll take Dave with me. He grew up in sun-kissed Australia."

Before Dave could argue his selection, Chuck had a valid point to make. "Hold up. What's your plan?"

"Ah, yes," Jimmy said, "I was thinking about this on the way down. I am Jimmy Jones, the famous journalist from Earth, and—"

"Are you going to tell them that?" Eddie asked.

"Yes. So I will go out with Dave and Cameron. The orb stays on the ship. I pretend I'm doing an article on Count Mein's amazing research. We don't know if he's here, but I'll wiggle my way into an audience with someone important. I have a way with people."

Dave rolled his eyes. "So why do you need me? I don't have any way with people."

"Just in case the people I have a way with aren't on Akalam. Plus, I may need your help in case things go sour. You heard Sowenso—the Count sounds a bit shifty. We need to be on guard, and the sight of a bodybuilder might make them think twice about trying anything."

"But I'm not a bodybuilder. I'm an accountant."

Jimmy looked him up and down. "Your arms are as thick as my thighs. You're a bodybuilder. Oh, don't worry. They're all historians and archaeologists out there. They'll wet themselves the moment they see you."

Dave sighed. "Fine."

"Good. Cameron will record everything he sees. Every artefact, every open book, every work of art, every building dug out of the ground. Make sure you listen to everything everyone says. We need as much information as possible."

"Will do," Cameron said.

Chuck cleared his throat. "They're probably wondering who we are, so let's not waste any more time. Remember, get in, learn as much as you can, and get out."

"Yes, boss."

Jimmy and Dave took the insufferably slow elevator down to change into their enviro suits. Cameron followed them and had to be told repeatedly by Dave that, no, he didn't want this part of the mission documented, and yes, he already knew what he looked like without clothes, and no, he didn't want a record of nude Jimmy. He'd already seen Jimmy moon people eight times, and that was eight too many.

"Ever climbed a volcano before?" Jimmy asked once they were in the airlock.

"No," Dave replied. "Seems a bit dangerous to me."

"Nothing to it. You can climb up to the top of some and look right into the opening. Gee, I hope none of these volcanoes erupt while we're here. Or an earthquake—that would suck too."

Dave closed his eyes, wishing his friend would shut up about life-ending scenarios. *Liberty*'s door opened and Akalam's low sun shone into the airlock. Their visors quickly adjusted to the lighting.

"Here goes," Jimmy said. "Look. Someone's coming to meet us already."

They descended the gangway to the ashy surface and waved at the approaching vehicle. It was an all-terrain explorer with huge infero-lifts holding it half a metre above the ground. A figure stepped out.

"Hello there," Jimmy called.

The person, who was clearly human, stayed put. His voice sounded slightly mechanical through his helmet's external speaker. "Who are you? What are you doing here?"

A man with tanned skin and dark eyebrows studied them from the other side of a clear helmet visor.

"I'm JayJay Jones, a freelance journalist, and this is David Ben Winklestein, my understudy. We're here to learn about the Akalam dig so the whole galaxy can know what awesome discoveries are being made."

Dave winced at the Judaification of his name. It was an ongoing joke that because he was an accountant and good with money, then he must have some Jewish blood in him. He liked a lighthearted, stereotypical joke every now and then and often made fun of his own Australianisms, but the guys just wouldn't give up the Jew jokes. Jimmy was the worst for it, always having a dig at him (no archaeology pun in intended). Which was why Dave never stopped dishing out the Irish ones.

"While my friend Jimmy here was blind drunk the other night," Dave said, "he hit his head and had a vision of Ancient Egypt. A pharaoh drinking a stout told him to learn about alien cultures. Now he wants to write an article on xenoarchaeology. So here we are."

Jimmy turned and looked at Dave, then faced their Akalam host. "Yes. And who do we have the pleasure of meeting?"

"I'm Doctor Shay Shahidi, chief historian here." He eyed Cameron who floated between Jimmy and Dave's heads. "I'll take you to Doctor Flemkoff. She's the one in charge here." He gestured for them to join him in the off-roader.

Dave closed his external speaker and spoke to Jimmy privately through an internal channel. "Way to go on the disguises, genius. They'll never figure out who we really are."

"I know, right," Jimmy replied.

"Huh?" Shahidi asked.

Dave grumbled. Jimmy had forgotten to turn off his external speaker.

"Oh, my understudy was just remarking how hot it is here."

"The external temperature is seventy-nine degrees Celsius," Cameron said.

They climbed into the off-roader and Shahidi did a one-eighty-degree spin before speeding back to the village.

"Yes," Shahidi said, "it is certainly horrible here, though it's an archaeologist's dream. How did you learn about this place, anyway?"

"A journalist never reveals his sources."

"Whatever you say." Shahidi clammed up after that.

Dave told Jimmy to shut off his external speaker, which Jimmy dutifully did this time. "What did Professor Sowenso say his missing friend's name was?"

Jimmy stared out the off-roader's windshield, then glanced at their driver. "Shahidi!"

"This is Sowenso's friend, the missing historian. Looks like he's gone over to Count Mein. Should we tell him about Sowenso?"

Jimmy thought about it for so long Dave wondered if he should ask the question again.

"No," Jimmy said finally. "That might cause us problems. Follow my lead." He opened his external speaker again and spoke to Shahidi. "So what's a historian doing in an archaeologist's dream?"

Shahidi snorted a laugh. "That sounds like the start of a joke. My employer has . . . special processes for studying history. He likes to keep his historians and archaeologists close. It improves collaboration."

"And what exactly are you studying here?" Jimmy asked.

They passed two giant energy generators and entered the village proper. "I'll leave that discussion to Doctor Flemkoff."

The buildings within the village were all prefabricated designs, probably dropped in huge crates and assembled automatically by bots before the archaeological team arrived. They had steep roofs, presumably to keep the ash from piling up. Bots cleaned the ash heaps that had piled up under the eaves between each building.

"I bet ash is a real problem here," Jimmy probed.

"It was yesterday," Shahidi replied. He turned sharply in what was most likely the village centre. "There is a line of active volcanoes a few hundred kilometres away, and we had a bad wind pushing the ash over us yesterday."

"Bet that upsets the archaeologists," Dave said. "You know, after all the digging and cleaning they do."

"Probably. I don't go down to the dig site, and I keep to myself up here."

Shahidi stopped abruptly in front of a large prefab

building. Frosted plastiglass glowed yellow and silhouettes moved about inside. Two people dressed in bright orange enviro suits stumbled out and descended the stairs, then wandered off in different directions, though they both had trouble putting one foot in front of the other.

"This is our drinking hole. You can wait here while I find Doctor Flemkoff. Come on, I'll introduce you to Bex."

When Dave stepped out of the off-roader, his enviro suit took a moment to readjust its internal temperature. A red light flashed next to the tavern door and Shahidi waited. It turned green and opened automatically. This time, three people emerged, one of whom bumped into Jimmy.

"Who the hell are you?" asked a slurred voice.

"I'm Batman," Jimmy replied in his best gravelly American accent.

"Whoa," was all the guy could say before one of his friends pulled him away.

"Day shift," Shahidi explained. "They work in the dig site all day, then drink all night." He prodded them into an entry chamber.

"Is it night-time?" Dave asked, for the sun was still shining its hot rays, albeit only a few degrees above the horizon.

"It is. We have perpetual daylight here in the northern hemisphere. The planet sits on a weird axis."

"It could have something to do with the tectonic activity," Cameron noted.

"You're a very perceptive little bot, aren't you?" Shahidi noted quietly.

"Oh, where are my manners?" Jimmy said. "This is Cameron. He is my flying encyclopaedia."

Shahidi nodded as though he didn't care and punched another button. The entry door closed and a timer appeared above another door opposite. Then a powerful vacuum system blasted them with air, blowing off ash and dust and sucking it through vents in the ceiling. The time still ticked as their suits were sprayed with a light blue vapour, then washed and dried by torrents of water and air.

After that thorough cleaning, the next timer reached zero, another light went green, and Shahidi pushed a button. The door slid open to a large, brightly-lit interior filled with tables. Most of the patrons wore orange, but a few others wore other colours. One or two were dressed similarly to Shahidi. A wall of crates had been stacked in a line and served as a bar. Behind it, a tall woman with a massive brunette beehive hairstyle stood polishing glasses. The chatter and music were a few decibels too loud for Dave but within an acceptable range for Jimmy.

They removed their helmets, and the guys got their first proper glimpse at Doctor Shahidi. Clean shaven, dark eyes and close-cropped black hair—he had the face of a movie star. At first impression, Jimmy thought he was quite young for a historian, but maybe he had good genes. He had not one wrinkle on his face, but though he had such a youthful appearance, his expressions and mannerisms were character-istic of a middle-aged man. He didn't smile.

Shahidi took them to the bar. "Bex, I bring visitors."

The tavern manager looked up from a spotless glass and cast a long smile at Shahidi, then regarded his followers. She gave Jimmy a polite glance and a nod, but her eyes brightened when she saw Dave. Dave, of course, was oblivious to this difference.

"Well, well," Bex cooed, "did you say visitors?"

Shahidi nodded.

"What are visitors? We don't get those around here."

"I thought the same," Shahidi said. "May I introduce . . . I seem to have forgotten your names."

Jimmy stepped forward and shook Bex's hand. "JayJay Jones and David Ben Winkleburg."

"Winklestein," Dave corrected. He leaned closer to Shahidi and whispered, "All the drinking has killed too many brain cells."

Bex withdrew her hand from Jimmy as quickly as she could and grasped Dave's, holding on for longer than the two seconds Dave usually permitted for a handshake. "A pleasure to meet you," she said, looking straight at Dave. "I'm Rebecca. Becky for short. Bex to a select few. You can call me Bex."

Dave pulled his hand away. "Nice place you have here."

"Bex," Shahidi said, "I'm going to leave our guests here while I find Doctor Flemkoff. Can you keep them company?"

Bex planted two glasses on the table. "Can do."

"Thank you." Then, to the guys. "Please make yourselves comfortable here, but watch the workers in orange. They can get a bit rowdy once they've had a few drinks."

They thanked him and he left. Bex poured them a drink she said was popular in the settlement and then disappeared into a back room to fetch some food.

Dave kept his voice low. "You think Shahidi knows about the blue orb?"

Jimmy checked that nobody was in earshot. "Nah. There's no way news could have reached here that fast. I didn't see any long-range comm systems."

"They could have sent a message via ship. *Liberty*'s fast, but she's not the fastest in the galaxy. Someone could have got here before us."

"True. I say we be on guard. I haven't seen anything shady here so far, but that doesn't mean we're in the clear."

"We're surrounded by Count Mein's people," Dave pointed out. "This is his operation."

"Yeah. But I know for certain that he's not here. Otherwise, Shahidi would be fetching Mein, not Flemkoff."

"I say we have a fifty-fifty chance of being pounced on by Mein's minions. We had a narrow escape at Onishi."

"There are twenty-one patrons in this tavern," Cameron told them. "Twelve are human, and the other nine are of various non-human races."

"Okay," Jimmy said. "Keep your eyes peeled. If we see trouble, we run back to *Liberty* and get the hell out of here. She's coming."

Bex returned with steaming plates of meat and vegetables. "Here you go, boys. Nuked some freeze-dried rations for you. How are the drinks?"

Dave hadn't tried it yet, so he sipped. It fizzed on his tongue and burned his throat, but the alcoholic aftertaste was sweet. "It's good."

Bex smiled and started polishing another glass. Jimmy asked her all sorts of questions, trying to learn as much as possible about Akalam and the dig site. Dave, on the other hand, fretted about Count Mein's goons possibly barging into the tavern at any moment, or even forcing their way onto *Liberty*. He sipped the alcoholic drink again to calm his nerves, but they were not soothed so easily.

7

ELASTIC JAWS

Every time new patrons arrived, a big green light would signal that the decontamination process had finished and that they were free to enter the tavern. Dave kept an eye on that light and tensed every time the big door hissed open. He expected faceless guards in black enviro suits armed with guns or truncheons or some other murderous and/or body-disfiguring implement.

Instead, about an hour after he'd left, Shahidi returned with a tall, thin person in a khaki-coloured enviro suit. They removed their helmets. The other person was a pale woman with a short blonde bob cut and striking blue eyes. Even before Shahidi pointed her to their guests, she had spotted Dave and locked eyes with him. Dave gulped and tapped Jimmy as they walked over.

"Gentlemen, I present Doctor Reta Flemkoff," Shahidi said.

She shook Dave's hand first. Even through both their gloves he could feel her bony fingers. But she held his gaze with an intensity he had never seen before. He wondered what she was thinking.

"Pleased to meet you, Doctor," Jimmy said loudly. He held out his hand, and Flemkoff was courteous enough to shake his too.

"Pray tell why one very handsome man and one long-haired lout have come to my quiet corner of the galaxy," Flemkoff said.

"We have come to learn about your dig site," Jimmy explained, "so we can write an article about your amazing research."

"And who are you to be writing articles about obscure archaeological expeditions?"

"I am JayJay Jones, a freelance journalist from Earth."

"Oh, the famous Jimmy Jones from *The Galactic Herald*!"

Jimmy was slightly taken aback by this statement and scolded himself for not thinking of a better alter ego. Since she had clearly identified him, he figured there was no sense denying the truth. "Yes and no. I quit so I could work on my own."

"I see." Flemkoff raised her eyebrows and looked longingly at Dave. "And your friend here?"

"I'm David."

"David . . . ?"

A pause. Dave's mind raced. What were the odds that she would know about a former low-level accountant from Sremmacs & Co, an insignificant firm? "David Ben Winklestein."

"Ah, German?"

"Um, sure, on my father's father's father's father's side."

Flemkoff's eyes twinkled just a little less. "I see. So, not German anymore?"

"One hundred per cent Aussie."

"Oh, too bad." She clapped her gloved hands together. "How can I help the esteemed Jimmy Jones?"

"Tell me everything about this marvellous dig site," Jimmy said excitedly. "I've heard great things about Count Mein's expeditions. I want to tell the whole galaxy about the wonders of a lost civilisation and the people exploring it."

"Of course, of course!" Flemkoff held her arms out wide. "Come with me, dear friends. I'll tell you everything."

They filled a table near the bar, away from the other patrons. Bex left them some glasses and a selection of colourful beverages. Cameron hovered nearby, secretly recording the scene.

"So, where shall we begin?" Flemkoff asked.

"Maybe let's start with Count Mein," Jimmy said. He opened his digipad. "How did you meet him, and why did he start digging on Akalam?"

That double-barrelled question kicked off a long monologue from Flemkoff about her life. She began with her early years as a xenoarchaeologist in Germany, her many experiences as a student and her junior field work on other planets. She explained in detail the nuances of her role, what distinguished her from her peers, and why she was the best choice to lead the Akalam dig. Nearly ten minutes later, she had mentioned barely two sentences about Count Mein or the specific reasons for exploring Akalam.

Jimmy made no notes. "Okay. Cool. What can you tell me about Akalam itself? What are you discovering from your activities here?"

Flemkoff launched into an excited lecture about Akalam's climate, its desolate landscape, the beauty of the lava seas, the relentless ash storms, and, of course, the heat. She remarked that it was lonely at times, and cast an enticing look at Dave, who missed the unspoken gesture entirely. Then she listed, in general terms, the knowledge they were gaining from the dig site: it was an old city, it was mostly destroyed, and there were no biological remains.

Hiding his dissatisfaction, Jimmy tried a different tactic. "You mentioned the volcanoes and the ash and that you have dug deep into the ground to find this old city. Do you know what happened here?"

"Yes. A massive volcanic eruption."

As soon as she said it, Jimmy realised he had already known the answer. Of course the city was buried in ash and pumice. Maybe a more direct question would work better. "What do you know about the people who lived here?"

"We know nothing. *Nothing.*"

This was the first time Dave had seen Jimmy as a journalist, and it sucked. It didn't suck like dropping the ice cream from your cone before after only one lick; no, it was more like being set on fire, then accidentally rolling off a cliff while trying to extinguish yourself, and on the way down being struck by lightning not once, but twice. It was *that* kind of suck. And because it sucked so bad, Dave knew Doctor Flemkoff was purposefully avoiding the specifics of the Hajari Kingdom. He cast a pleading face at Shahidi, but the historian casually watched Jimmy and Flemkoff dancing through their pointless interview.

Jimmy downed a big gulp of some steaming drink that had a strong whiff of ethanol. He glared at his empty digipad and proceeded with the interview.

"Have you found anything useful or interesting in the dig site?"

"Not really."

"Are there any other dig sites like this in the galaxy?"

"Not sure."

"Do you find my friend attractive?"

"Yes."

"Why is Count Mein so interested in the Hajari Kingdom?"

"He likes history."

"What is it about Hajari history he finds so interesting?"

"Mainly the stories."

"What stories can you tell me from Hajari history?"

"None. We don't know the beginnings or the ends. Only the middle."

"How would you summarise your expedition here on Akalam?"

"Sweaty."

Jimmy nodded, closed his digipad to its portable pen size, and pocketed it. "I think we're done here."

"Marvellous!" Her face beamed as she stood and shook their hands. "I've so enjoyed talking to you. You were a welcome reprieve from the everyday boredom of this broken planet. Do let me know when the article goes live." She checked a watch built into the wrist of her enviro suit. "Ah, but I must be off. Shay will keep you company for the rest of your stay here."

Flemkoff picked up her helmet, gave one last look at Dave, sighed, and made for the door. Dave and Jimmy exchanged a glance, though for entirely different reasons.

While Jimmy thought, *You lucky dog*, Dave thought, *We've just wasted our time*.

"Will you spend the night?" Shahidi asked. "I suppose you could sleep on your ship."

Dave put both palms on the table, readying himself to stand. "No, I don't think there is anything more for us to do here."

"I agree." Jimmy said.

"I understand," Shahidi said, nodding. "I can't blame you for wanting to leave this hellhole."

"It certainly is a hole," Jimmy mumbled. "But you have been quite hospitable, and we will not forget it."

They all stood and crisscrossed the table in an awkward episode of handshakes. Caught up in the confusion, even Dave and Jimmy shook hands. Shahidi offered to drive them back to their ship.

"Nah, don't worry," Jimmy said. He aimed a thumb at Dave. "He needs the exercise."

Shahidi reluctantly let them go. They wished him well with his research and hoped the Akalam dig would turn up some good results soon.

In the decontamination chamber, Jimmy let loose.

"Oh, I've been holding that in for ages!" he said. "Must've been that drink."

"You couldn't do it outside?" Dave asked, frantically attaching his helmet."

"Best place for it here. These vacuums will take the smell right away."

They endured a different process in the chamber this time. Since they were leaving the safety of the tavern and re-entering the big, bad desolate world outside, the chamber adjusted atmospheric parameters, gradually heating up so their enviro suits could match what awaited them when the exit door opened. They had gone through a similar process in *Liberty*'s chamber a few hours earlier.

When they stepped out to the dull wasteland, it was Dave's turn to let it rip, except he used words. "So what the hell happened in there?"

"We got a bum steer, that's what," Jimmy told him.

They marched along the pumice road. It flicked up with each step, caking their boots.

"I recorded a great deal of biographical material," Cameron said.

Jimmy scoffed. "And I think I just received a commission to write Flemkoff's biography."

"A waste of time."

Jimmy stopped in his tracks and scanned the area. "Follow me." And he was off.

Dave hurried in his wake. "Where are we going?"

"To look at the dig site."

Jimmy moved with purpose, weaving between prefab buildings and towards an entry point to the dig site—an empty guard box with controls for a nearby elevator platform.

"We're clear," Jimmy said when they were halfway there.

Two helmeted heads appeared, followed by shoulders and the rest of two bodies, rising on the platform, returning from the dig site. They were tall enviro-suited figures with blacked-out visors. Something clearly designed to kill or maim people hung from their hips.

Without slowing down, Jimmy did a full one-eighty and retraced his path, collecting Dave and Cameron along the way.

"Yeah, we're not getting down there," he said. "Forget it."

"So we've definitely wasted this whole trip," Dave replied.

"Mmhmm."

They walked in silence the whole way back to *Liberty*. Akalam's star cast a perpetual orange glow on the landscape. Its low position cast obscene shadows across their path, but at least it broke the monotony of bare grey pumice.

Still about a hundred metres from *Liberty*'s gangway, they heard the loud roar of a vehicle behind them. An off-roader gunned it along the hard volcanic rock surface.

"Cameron," Dave started, "get inside."

"Act casual," Jimmy said as the drone zoomed away.

Dave stayed ready to leg it back to *Liberty*. He knew Jimmy could almost keep pace with him, so if things turned sour, they might be okay. Then he paled. Unless Count Mein's people had already stormed *Liberty*!

"Eddie, you there?" he asked through his helmet's radio unit.

No reply came the answer.

"Chuck?"

Again, silence.

The off-roader stopped in a cloud of ash.

"They are playing football in the lounge," Eve chimed in. "Man United versus Man City."

"Who's winning?" Jimmy asked. There was so much ash in the air that he couldn't see Dave's incredulous face in response to the question.

"Man U by one. But Chuck is about to take a free kick to even the score."

Through the ash cloud, someone approached and stopped just far enough away that they could see an outline, but no discernible features. Jimmy wondered if it was Count Mein himself.

"I wanted to speak to you before you left," said a familiar voice. The ash cleared in a hot wind and the figure stepped closer. It was Shahidi. "I'm glad I met you—both of you—if only briefly."

The guys stood in awkward silence.

Shahidi reached for Jimmy's hand and they bid each other farewell again. But this time, the haptic sensors in Jimmy's glove felt something more than a hand. Jimmy held whatever it was, but closed his hand into a fist to hide it.

"Be careful out there," Shahidi said. "And good luck." He about-faced and made for the off-roader.

Jimmy opened his hand and saw a piece of torn paper with a handwritten note. "Why?" he asked.

Shahidi halted and spoke with his back to them, looking at the barren ground. "I used to work for an old xenologist. If he knew I'd met you and didn't do anything to right my wrongs . . . I don't know. I couldn't face him, if I ever get to see him again. I just want to do the right thing, and you're my only option."

"You'll see Doctor Sowenso again," Jimmy told him.

Shahidi turned his head, half looking at them over his shoulder. "You've met him?"

"We have."

Shahidi sighed and looked at the ground again. "I don't

know how you are mixed up with the Hajari, but watch your-selves out there. Count Mein sees and hears everything."

He hurried to the off-roader, gave them one last glance, and drove off towards the village.

Jimmy examined the note again. "Let's get out of here. We have our next clue."

8

RING RACE

The airlock equalised the atmosphere and ran through the decontamination process. Once Jimmy and Dave peeled off their enviro suits and left them in the storage compartment, they took the elevator up, eager to tell Eddie and Chuck about how nothing happened on their excursion into the wasteland of Akalam.

Except something did happen.

Dave saw the note in Jimmy's hand while they rode the elevator. "What's that?"

"Shahidi gave it to me. It's our next clue."

"What's it say?"

"I don't know." He showed Dave. "It looks Arabic."

Dave studied it with furrowed brows. "Could be."

"You think Cameron can translate it?"

"Most likely." Dave sighed. "Is that why he went on about Sowenso and feeling sorry for himself?"

"Yeah. I guess this is his way of making amends. But we won't be fixing anything unless we can get this translated."

They rode the rest of the slow elevator trip (up one deck) in silence.

"Did you enjoy your sojourn?" Eve asked as the elevator door opened.

"No," Dave said.

"The other two are in a penalty shootout, two to three."

Jimmy went straight to the lounge and stood in front of the vidscreen, arms out, exasperated, just as Chuck's player was taking a penalty kick. The shot went wide, Chuck shouted angrily at Jimmy, Eddie laughed victoriously, and Dave went for a beer.

"What are you doing?" Chuck bellowed. "You cost me the game!"

"It would have been a draw anyway," Eddie said. "How did it go out there?"

"It sucked," Dave said from the bar.

"Yes, it did suck," Jimmy added, "but we met Professor Sowenso's lost historian, and he gave us this." He handed them the note.

"Klingon?" Eddie wondered.

Chuck tutted and shook his head. "It's Farsi. Plenty of Iranians where I lived in London."

Jimmy retrieved the note. "Cameron, can you translate Farsi?"

The camera bot whizzed into the room and studied the note. He was silent for some time. "Oh, I see now. The nouns are spelled out phonetically. Perhaps there was no way to convert them to Farsi. The note reads: FIND THE OLD HAG IN SCARLETVILLE ON RUBICUND. *Rubicund* means *red* or *reddish in appearance*."

"It is also the name of a planet in my star charts," Eve said. "The capital of which is Scarletville."

Jimmy clapped. "Right. Sounds like we're searching for a pub on a red planet. Raise anchor and set sail. We're going to Rubicund!"

"Eve, start the engine and lift off, please," Eddie translated. He'd barely finished the sentence before the boom of thrusters vibrated through the ship.

The guys darted to the cockpit. Dave downed his beer first because Eddie had banned all drinks from the cockpit ever since Chuck spilled iced coffee. Once they were strapped in, Eve punched it towards space, leaving the hot, drab, volcanic Akalam behind.

"I'm picking up a signal from orbit," Eve said.

"That's weird," Eddie said. "I don't remember any satellites."

When *Liberty* came within range, Eve plotted the signal on the navigational map.

"It's a ship in geosynchronous orbit over the village," she explained. "There are minor thruster bursts keeping it in position."

They left Akalam's atmosphere, and the sky turned star-studded black. The planet's ring hung some distance away, a bright, deep line of rock, ice, and dust. The other ship sat off to starboard, growing in size as *Liberty* carved a power-hungry run at escape velocity. Any change in course now would require more power to leave Akalam's gravitational pull, which was surprisingly strong.

"Could this ship be one of the mining vessels we saw earlier?" Chuck asked.

"Different signal," Eve said. "Look! It's moving. It's cutting across our path."

"I'm hailing them," Eddie said.

"Why not just run for it?" Dave asked.

"We need a straight or slightly angled exit from the planet," Eddie explained. "Otherwise, the gravity will suck too much power. We're still too close to change course."

Eddie sent a message out over a general frequency. "Oi, you're obstructing our exit. Get out of the way."

Chuck cleared his throat. "Say 'please'."

"Please."

The ship veered even more sharply into *Liberty*'s path.

"They've sent a file to us," Eve announced.

"Maybe they're aliens and this is the only way they can communicate," Jimmy suggested.

"No, wait," Eddie said. "Eve, don't open it. Cameron, can you work some magic on that file? See what it is without opening it?"

Cameron buzzed over to a terminal and jacked in. The little yellow flying ball was a powerfully jailbroken machine, thanks to its previous owner. Cameron could hack into just about anything without any regard to privacy or safety. The guys remembered their near-death experience all too well— Cameron tried to suffocate them all and escape with Eve and *Liberty*. That was before he underwent the programming knife and was re-written by Eve.

"This file contains a well-hidden virus," Cameron said. "It would have shut Eve down in seconds and rendered the entire ship inoperable."

The guys exchanged glances, nodded, then said in unison, "Count Mein."

Eddie hummed like a computer, a sure sign that he was

thinking. "Cameron, can you re-purpose that virus somehow?"

"Sure I can. What do you have in mind? Engine plant meltdown? Life support system malfunction? Overriding autopilot and setting a collision course for the sun?"

"We don't want to kill them! Can you shut down their engines?"

"If you insist."

"Can you send the virus as an invitation to open a video-link? Maybe add a request for a parley."

"On it."

The opposing ship was now directly in their path and closing in fast. It was narrower than *Liberty* and had the look of a fast space yacht, not unlike the one Chuck lost to his wife during their divorce. If it was Count Mein's people, then they were hunting the guys in complete luxury.

"I could try ploughing into them," Eve suggested, "but it won't look pretty."

Eddie's face paled. "Eve, I'm taking direct control." He grabbed the helm and wondered how he got saddled with two maniacal AIs.

They had nearly reached the safe zone for a course change, but they were also so close to the other ship that they could see an outline of its pilot through the cockpit window.

"How much longer, Cameron?" Eddie asked.

"Not long."

"How long?"

"Five minutes."

"We're going to crash," Dave cried out. "Why am I always the only one saying that?"

Eddie checked the distance from Akalam. "We're not

crashing today." He turned hard to port and gunned it towards Akalam's ring.

Dave let out a yelp and gripped his armrests and Jimmy cheered.

Chuck kept an eye on the 3D map. "They're following."

Eddie, who had a smaller map display next to the helm, acknowledged the observation. His days as an illegal 'roid racer flushed his memory. Back then, as a teenager scooting around predetermined paths among asteroid fields, he had piloted smaller, faster vessels—too small to be called ships. His situation now was different, given *Liberty*'s size. She was, however, unusually fast for her mass, and he used that to his advantage. He'd put a good distance between them and the pursuing ship, but it began to close the gap.

"Let's see how they like rocks."

Liberty screamed through the middle of Akalam's ring. The rocks were much smaller than asteroids, which made them more dangerous to navigate. *Liberty*'s spotted orange as smaller rocks and dust particles were incinerated on impact.

"You want me to help?" Eve asked.

"Nah," Eddie said. "I need manual control for this."

"Please let Eve fly," Dave begged as a bead of sweat ran down his forehead.

Eddie craned his neck to look around his pilot's chair as a stressed-out father would in a car on a family holiday. A space rock, too large to be fully incinerated, passed through the shield and bounced off *Liberty*'s bow as he spoke.

"I have raced through rings before," Eddie assured him. "I know what I'm doing."

Dave gasped and pointed ahead, and Eddie had just enough time to dodge a gigantic rock big enough to land on. Jimmy laughed, and from then on Dave kept his eyes closed and used up his year's quota of prayers.

The yacht was now hot on their tail, matching *Liberty*'s speed and manoeuvres. Eddie didn't want to cause any accidents, which made his job that much more difficult. He was unsure of the other pilot's skill, so he was hesitant to go too close to the rocks. If he performed enough wild antics, though, perhaps the pursuer would back off. To Dave's dismay, Eddie barrel-rolled *Liberty*, twisting and turning, hugging the largest rocks.

Deeper into the ring, large ice formations dominated. They shone brilliantly against the light of Akalam's sun, enough that Chuck felt compelled to remark, "Oh, it's beautiful." *Liberty* then completely obliterated one ice chunk, which was followed by a stern reprimand from Eve. Still, no matter how crazy Eddie flew, the yacht followed them like a bloodhound.

They soared over a long clump of ice and one of the mining vessels loomed in front. Large and ponderous, its pilot turned hard to starboard and dipped the bow to escape *Liberty*'s onrush. This raised its stern so high that even Eddie gasped when he reduced engine power and clawed at *Liberty*'s helm to dodge the obstruction.

"Missed it by forty-two millimetres," Eve noted calmly.

The 3D display visualised a second near miss as Count Mein's pilot nearly collided with the miner too. Since Eddie brought *Liberty* up so high, the yacht screamed by underneath, between *Liberty* and the mining vessel. Now the chaser was in front, and Eddie capitalised on the mistake. The yacht slowed and tilted upwards to begin a sharp inside loop, impressive for its size and style of craft.

"Got it!" Cameron said. "Shall I send the virus?"

"Yes, please!" Dave yelled, eyes closed, nursing a headache already.

"Do it, Cameron," Eddie said.

"Virus sent," Cameron announced a second later.

And just like that, the space yacht went dark and stopped mid-manoeuvre, pointing directly upwards. Its momentum carried it forth on an unstoppable drift out of Akalam's ring. Eddie brought *Liberty* to a standstill.

Cameron unjacked himself and looked out the cockpit window at his handiwork. "Target neutralised."

"What did you do to it?" Chuck asked.

"I cut all power for thirty minutes. It will drift without engines, no life support, and no way for the pilot to communicate. He's probably scrambling for his enviro suit right now."

"He won't suffocate, will he?" Eddie asked.

"Nah, that thing will have hours of available oxygen."

They sat there for a moment. Eddie's head tilted to the side. "Would his gravity stabiliser have been disabled as well?"

"Yep."

Eddie nodded. "So he'll be swimming through zero-grav. Can't be that bad."

"Can we leave now?" Dave asked impatiently.

"Yes," Jimmy agreed. "We've had our fun." He nudged Dave. "Off to Rubicund."

"We should fly to the other side of Akalam," Eve said. "When we enter FTL travel, Akalam will serve as a screen and hide our jump trajectory. Plus, I've been antagonising the AIs on the mining ships this whole time and they're really pissed now. They may take direct control of their ships and try to ram us."

"Off we go, then," Eddie said.

"Eat my space dust, mining mutts," Eve taunted audibly for the benefit of her human passengers.

Eddie took *Liberty* out of the rocky, icy ring system and skirted around Akalam. On the way, the guys got another sweeping view of the cracked and bleeding surface of a long-forgotten Hajari world.

Jimmy wondered why the Hajari would inhabit such a planet and guessed that they would be visiting plenty of dark, lava-covered ecosystems. He didn't mind, though, as long as there was treasure to be found, and as long as a certain German nobleman/archaeologist didn't thwart his adventure.

Liberty reached a jump point that Eve had plotted and Eddie engaged the FTL drive, launching the ship on the next leg of their journey—to Rubicund, in search of The Old Hag and answers to their many questions.

Thirty minutes later, the yacht's power supply came back online. The pilot, fully dressed in an enviro suit, dropped to the deck as the gravity stabiliser corrected itself. The hard deck became the floor once again. He rubbed both his knees, stood, and marched to the cockpit, removing his helmet on the way.

The first thing he did was turn towards Akalam. He shook his head when he saw how far from the ring he'd drifted.

Those idiots in the watermelon ship had done him a good one with that virus—they'd used his own strategy against him.

He punched some buttons and opened a long-distance audiolink.

"You have an update?"

The pilot sighed. "My lord, I'm calling from Akalam. I'm sorry, but by the time I received your sortie order and flew here, they were already on the surface."

Of course, he failed to mention that when the order reached him, he was halfway through a rather lascivious evening with another of his lord's agents, and they may have ignored the urgent order for a few hours.

"Do not worry yourself," a calm voice replied. "Doctor Flemkoff contacted me and kept them busy until you arrived. Have they left the planet yet?"

The pilot took a deep breath. "Uh, yes, my lord."

"So you have them?"

"No, my lord. They . . . escaped. They disabled my ship and escaped behind Akalam. I do not know which direction they went. I'm . . . sorry."

The voice grumbled and sighed through the ship's speakers. "Who are these people? Regardless, it's an inconsequential hiccup. By now, we have every planet of interest monitored in orbit and on the surface. They will appear again, and when they do, we will move in."

"Very good, my lord. What are your orders for me?"

"I want you to go down to Akalam and ask Flemkoff what happened. I want to compare her story with yours."

"As you command."

"And, Baldrick . . . ?"

"Yes, my lord?"

"Don't fall in the lava. It's not healthy."

9

RANDOM ENCOUNTER

CHUCK PACED THE LOUNGE room, scratching his chin. Jimmy sat at the bar writing notes about Akalam with the help of Cameron's recordings. Eddie claimed the couch and drank a beer while reading a user manual for some obscure mechanical contraption he would never own. Dave busied himself with the pinball machine, but assured Chuck he was listening.

"So, let's recap," Chuck said. "We go to Akalam, and they don't let you into the dig site."

"Correct," Jimmy said while typing.

"They make no mention whatsoever about orbs or the Hajari Kingdom."

"Correct the second."

"They make no offer to introduce you to Count Mein."

"Correct the third."

Chuck stood with his hands behind his back. "Okay. And now we're going to a planet neither of us have visited, and we're to find 'The Old Hag'. Any ideas on what that might be?"

"Pub."

"Pub."

"Pub."

"Are you all just saying 'pub' because you want to drink on a new planet?"

"Yes."

"No."

"Yes."

Chuck shrugged, pulled a beer out of the fridge, and joined Eddie on the couch. But as he raised the bottle to his lips, an old man materialised in the middle of the room. Everyone else was too distracted to notice. Chuck stared, his mouth hovering over the open beer bottle. The old man stared back. He had voluminous white hair that reached past his shoulders and a big, curious eye. A large ocular mechanism covered the other eye.

The old man scanned the room, then glanced at a device in his hand. "It worked!"

The shout made Eddie jump, spilling his beer. Dave flinched and accidentally let the pinball slip past the flippers. Jimmy nearly fell off his bar stool.

The old man smiled widely and looked at each of the guys, like how a bird snaps its head to-and-fro. He laughed madly. "It worked!"

He fiddled with his device and dematerialised, leaving behind a white busine ss card that floated to the deck.

"Did everyone see that?" Chuck asked.

Everyone nodded.

Dave picked up the card and read it aloud. "'D. Kratz, Spatiotemporal Inventor & Air Conditioning Mechanic'."

"Did we just receive a visit from a time traveller?" Eddie asked.

Dave reread the card a few more times. "A space *and* time traveller, it would seem."

Chuck squeezed his eyes shut. "My brain cannot comprehend what just happened."

"Yes, that was weird," Jimmy conceded. "Anyway, we can deal with that after we find my treasure. Back to the issue at hand: we have no idea what's in store for us at Rubicund."

Dave pocketed the business card. He made a mental note to remove it before washing his pants, then, remembering that he never remembered mental notes, set a reminder on his digipad. "And that historian told us to be careful. Sowenso said the same."

"All right," Eddie said. He finished his beer. "We'll be careful. But if this Count Mein wants us dead, I won't let him catch us alive. Right, Eve?"

"Right, Eddie. You'll be dead before he catches you."

"Damn right." Eddie went to the lounge room viewport, the very same viewport through which Jimmy once mooned a dangerous band of mercenaries. "But if I'm flying into danger, I'm glad it's with you guys."

Chuck, sufficiently recovered from his shock, raised his bottle. "I'll drink to that."

Jimmy stood and slapped the bar. "Yeah. Whatever Rubicund throws at us, it'll be no match for us." He fetched a beer for himself and picked out an Australian one for Dave. Cracking it open, he triumphantly said, "To Count Mein's orbs!"

The guys cheered and rode on a high all the way to Rubicund. What dangers awaited them? They didn't know. Did they care? Not in the slightest. Did it matter? Probably.

10

ARRIVAL AT SCARLETVILLE

Every planet is beautiful to someone, but few planets are beautiful to everyone. *Liberty* exited FTL drive not far out from Rubicund, and the scene greeting the guys was absolutely breathtaking. It was possibly the most vibrant planet any of them had ever seen. Deep red continents stretched around the equator, turning pink in the higher and lower latitudes, before ending in frozen white poles. Bodies of blue-green ocean broke up the landmasses, and small wisps of clean white clouds flitted about.

"Well, this looks fine, indeed," Chuck said.

"It's like a communist's wet dream," Jimmy added.

Rubicund had no orbiting or moon-based spaceport. Instead, a flight controller from Scarletville told them to dock at one of the large ground-based ports. They headed towards a sprawling grey patch that was dotted red and pink and split down the middle by a blue river.

It seemed the designers of Scarletville had tried to keep Rubicund's signature red theme for the capital city, and not just in name. As they neared, the guys noticed red flowering trees lining the streets and vermilion gardens populating many rooftops. Several large buildings even had ruby-tinted roofs. Eddie said there was too much red, but for someone like Dave, who could appreciate the subtleties of colours and shades, the city borrowed from nature and cultivated its own beauty because of it. It was a wonderful change from Akalam.

The same flight controller directed them to a vacant lot at Scarletville Spaceport. It was a huge field of concrete, though the landing pads were divided by narrow, low-lying red hedges. Eddie ordered supplies and organised a cleaning crew to wipe up the giant, crusty bird droppings that still clung to the upper parts of *Liberty*'s hull, courtesy of the birds of Isthan.

"There is no local internet entry for 'The Old Hag'," Eve told them. "Sounds like you'll be doing a pub crawl. Try not to get so drunk that you have to crawl all the way back here."

"Only Jimmy and Chuck get drunk nowadays," Eddie said.

Jimmy, ignoring the jibe, zipped his orb vessel into a backpack and carried it over his shoulder. "Okay, so we ask the locals. Someone is bound to know something."

"I say we take a taxi," Chuck said. "My car is still covered in crap, and taxi drivers know where everything is."

They walked across the concrete to customs and had their identification checked, which was a much speedier process than at Onishi. Then they went to the taxi rank and marvelled at the variety of yellow and white vehicles waiting to be hired, all unique and personalised with chrome ornaments. They picked the first four-door they saw and climbed in.

The driver was a friendly girl with blonde dreadlocks who flashed a smile as they entered. "Where to?"

Jimmy sat in the front passenger seat, holding his backpack in his lap. He shrugged and decided to hit the ground running. "To The Old Hag, please."

"You got it," the driver said.

The guys exchanged glances as she joined the traffic.

"What can you tell us about The Old Hag?" Chuck asked from the back seat.

The driver waved a dismissive hand. "It's best if you find out for yourself. Then you can develop your own impressions."

She drove like a madwoman. The city wasn't all that busy, but their driver seemed to think that the quicker her fares arrived at their destination, the better. She weaved in and out of traffic, seemingly oblivious to any road rules. They came to an alley, which she said was a shortcut, but they were stopped halfway in by a garbage truck. After a few choice words between trucker and cabbie, she threw the taxi into reverse and backed up at speed.

"Oh, I hate going backwards," Dave said. His head spun.

"Just think of it as going forwards in reverse," she told him.

They burst out onto the street from which they'd come, and the cabbie seamlessly spun from reverse into a forwards direction and travelled along the busy thoroughfare until reaching a highway. Then, in true autobahn fashion, she let the taxi's engine roar delightfully and picked the fastest lanes.

"What do you have under the hood?" Eddie asked. "I used to be a racer."

"V8 twin-turbo," the driver replied.

"Nice."

"They let souped-up taxis zoom all over the city?" Dave asked.

"The taxi system on Rubicund is a partially-regulated industry," she explained. "Most drivers are sole proprietors. You need insurance, you need to be registered for tax, you need a safety certificate, and your car needs the government-mandated liveries of a taxi. But what vehicle you use and what modifications it has is entirely up to the driver. Take this one for example—"

A white and yellow supercar screamed past them, its large central exhaust burning red hot.

"That's Arlo," she went on. "He has room for only one passenger and little luggage, but he charges enough to make up for it. Plus, he'll reach his destination before pretty much anything else. Good for ferrying high-paying businesspeople to the spaceport Then you have something like that." She pointed to something akin to a family station wagon.

"All these taxis travelling at different speeds must give law enforcement a headache," Chuck said.

"No, not really. We have some road rules, but few speed limits. It all works somehow."

Conversation remained steady around the topic of cars and engines, so it was basically Eddie and the driver talking while the others listened. The city became suburbia—an inner neighbourhood with tall trees and old houses.

The driver pulled up outside a pale blue house. "We're here."

Jimmy twisted around, looking at the street. "Where's The Old Hag?"

The driver pointed. "There."

Sitting in a rocking chair on the porch of the pale blue house was a round, dark woman with frizzy white hair.

"That's The Old Hag?" Jimmy asked.

"Known from here to Crimsontown," the driver explained. "She's a bit of a local legend. Her name is Hagne, by the way."

"Ohhh," the guys said in unison.

"So she has the answers," Jimmy said, so quietly that it was probably to himself. "Let's go speak with her."

The taxi driver smirked. "Good luck."

11

HAGGLING

THE GUYS APPROACHED THE house. The old lady swayed back and forth on her rocking chair, staring off into oblivion. A couple walking a dog passed them, minding their own business.

Then Hagne piped up. "Don't step on the cracks in the sidewalk! You hear?"

The couple lowered their heads, hiding grins, and kept walking. Meanwhile, the guys stopped at her front gate.

"How did you lot get here?" she shouted. "Did someone leave your cages open? And you, get a haircut."

Jimmy absentmindedly brushed his long black hair. "Are you Hagne?"

"Who wants to know?"

"We do," Jimmy replied excitedly.

Chuck rolled his eyes. "We are Chuck, Eddie, Dave, and Jimmy. We were hoping to ask you some questions."

Hagne raised her chin. "Come to me."

They swung the creaky gate open and marched up the garden path to stand before her on the porch. She seemed to stare right through them, and only then did they realise that she was blind.

"You are not the only ones to come here looking for answers," she said. "Others have been here before you, but they were different. Grumpy. I sense something different now." She stood, knees popping, and pointed at Eddie. "You, the balding one."

Eddie planted a hand on his chest. "How did you know I'm balding?"

"Because I can hear the way the breeze rushes through your thinning hair. Did you close the gate after you entered?"

"Uh, no. Sorry, I'll close it." He toddled off.

"Animals!" Hagne said. "Humanity has become a sprawling den of animals. It's no wonder our race has stagnated. Follow me, and don't touch anything."

She led them inside, Eddie rushing back to join them and making sure to close the front door behind him. Her house was neat and clean, though Hagne insisted she had no help from family, friends, or housekeepers. Red-veined timber furniture complemented every room.

She took them to a sitting room with lavish chairs upholstered in pale pink material offsetting the natural red grain of a timber coffee table. On the coffee table was a thick book about tea, and atop the book was a coaster and a tall glass half-filled with water.

"Sit, sit," she beckoned. She dropped into a single armchair, while the four guys had to squeeze together on a three-seater lounge. "Now, what have you come to ask?" Her empty eyes gazed slightly above their heads.

They all nudged Jimmy to speak. He cleared his throat. "Well, I don't know what the question is, but we've discovered something from the Hajari Kingdom. We were pointed to you."

"Who pointed you to me?"

Jimmy looked at Chuck. As the lawyer, Chuck would have opinions on how much information to provide and what to hold back, but this time he just nodded. What harm could an old lady do?

"Doctor Shay Shahidi," Jimmy said.

Hagne smiled, closed her eyes, and nodded. "Ah, the nice one. He was apologetic about the way his colleagues questioned me. When they persisted, I shouted them down and told them not to come back."

"Why did they come here?" Chuck asked.

Hagne grinned and cast her unblinking gaze right at Chuck's face, which was slightly unnerving.

"Why did they come here?" Chuck repeated, though the command in his voice had waned somewhat.

"Because I have answers."

"And they knew you had answers?" Eddie asked.

"They knew I knew they knew I knew, but they didn't know I knew they didn't know they wouldn't get them."

Dave scratched his head, already lost.

Hagne heard the scratching. "Did I confuse you?"

"He's easily confused with words," Jimmy said. "So these people came here to ask you something. It was about the Hajari Kingdom?"

"Oh, yes. The Kingdom, and where they might find it. Is that what you want to know?"

"We do," Jimmy said.

"Why?"

Jimmy shrugged. "For discovery. For something to write about. For the adventure."

Hagne hummed approvingly. "And not for the untold wealth that the last Hajari king supposedly hoarded all to himself?" She cackled. "I may be old, but I'm not stupid. You are young men. You want the money. What will you do with such wealth? Money is not the be all and end all of life."

"We are rebuilding a city and repairing a biome that was destroyed by ecological disaster," Chuck explained. "Any wealth we find would go to that cause."

"Ah, so you are four noble men. And what do you get out of it? People seldom do good deeds without some repayment."

"We get to live in a paradise that was previously ruined by humans," Chuck said. "We get the satisfaction of righting a wrong inflicted by people who only cared about profit and leisure. And we make amends with a living planet that is kind enough to give humans a second chance."

Hagne chuckled. "Noble indeed. The others who came here, they wanted more than wealth. I think they already had enough money. No, they were after something that they couldn't get anywhere other than from the Hajari worlds."

"What did they want?" Jimmy asked.

She inclined her head to one side. "You have brought something with you, something . . . Hajari. Show it."

Jimmy opened his backpack and pulled out the orb vessel. "May I place it on the table?"

"Please do."

Jimmy put the vessel down and opened it. The orb floated free, but this time it not only glowed blue, but it pulsed with brilliant azure. The guys stared in astonishment at this new sight.

"An orb," Hagne said. "I can feel its presence. Where did you get it?"

"We found it in an antique shop," Jimmy answered.

"Hmm."

"How can you feel its presence?" Eddie asked. "I can't."

"Nor can I," Chuck added.

"Same," said Dave.

"Let's call it educated intuition," Hagne said. "And heightened senses due to the loss of my eyesight."

Jimmy leaned forward. "I can feel it. Is it the tingling under my skin? The goosebumps?"

Hagne stared at him. "No. You're cold."

She turned on the heating system with a remote, then sighed and dropped her head, closing her eyes. Her chest rose and fell with every breath, and for a moment the guys thought she may have fallen asleep. She opened her eyes and swept her blind gaze across them.

"I will help you," she said at last. "But first, you need to do something for me. You will dine with me tonight, for I want to introduce you to someone who can help you. He has a favourite meal—a special dish—but I need you to go to the supermarket and buy the ingredients for me."

Dave, ever the gentleman, sat upright. "Of course. Let's make a list."

"Oh, thank you, young man. I so dearly hate going to the supermarket—it's full of such idiotic people who lose all good sense once they're behind a shopping trolley. Here are the ingredients."

She rattled off twelve items, most of which the guys had never heard of. But if they were stocked in the local supermarket, as Hagne said, then the task shouldn't be that difficult.

"You had best be on your way," Hagne said. "I like to eat dinner at six, and the later you visit the shops, the more stupid the other customers get."

She pointed to Jimmy. "You, Irishman, you will stay here. I want to talk about your orb."

12

THE BIGGEST SUPERMARKET IN THE GALAXY

As MUCH AS DAVE disliked their cabbie's driving style, he reluctantly agreed to take the taxi to the supermarket. She'd waited outside Hagne's house, sprawled on her bonnet, soaking up the afternoon sun like a beach babe.

"Figured you guys might need another lift," she said as they approached. "You're down one."

"He's staying back," Eddie said. "Can you take us to the supermarket?"

"P-p-p . . ."

"Please?"

"Sure." She hopped off the bonnet and stretched. "Ashley, by the way. If I'm going to be your personal driver, you should at least know my name."

Dave shook her hand and felt auto grease between her fingers. "Fair enough. We'll be coming back here after the supermarket, but then we don't know for how long we'll be staying."

"That's okay. Just call me. The way I drive, I'll be here in a flash."

Dave bit his tongue. "Okay, we shouldn't keep Hagne

waiting." He immediately regretted his choice of words.

"Too right," Ashley said. "Let's bounce!"

Dave—unlucky man—had the front passenger seat where he could see every oncoming car, every darting pedestrian, and his whole life flashing before his eyes. His hands shook when he stepped out at the supermarket parking lot.

"See you soon, big guy," Ashley said, winking at him.

"How do you do it?" Chuck asked as they went through the huge glass supermarket doors.

"Do what?" Dave asked.

"Every woman melts around you."

"Do they?" he asked. His voice still quivered from the drive.

Eddie laughed. "It's your muscles. The girls love a meat head."

Chuck smacked his small belly with both hands, "Me, I'll stick to my dad-bod."

To call the supermarket a *super*market was an understatement. *Mega*market or *ultra*market was more appropriate. The guys stood at one end of Aisle Six and it was so long that the other end hid behind the curvature of the planet. The locals seemed to know where to go, and go they went. Shopping trolleys bumped into each other as customers flitted from one shelf to another, from one aisle to another, and blocked passageways while talking to friends, much to the dismay of other shoppers and the supermarket staff.

The aisles had side-by-side vidscreens displaying various news channels. The one closest to the guys showed a news team on one screen, gossiping about a news team from a rival network. The adjacent vidscreen had that rival news team, engaging in a similar activity about the first team. They were across the road from one another. Chuck shook his head and wondered what Jimmy would think of such pointless journalism.

"All right," Chuck said, "let's find these items. What's first?"

"One vial of Dismaran toe juice," Dave said, then slouched. "Is she for real?"

The others shrugged.

They hailed a passing worker and asked where they might find Dismaran toe juice—Chuck swallowed bile as he asked out loud—and were shocked when the worker said, "Of course, sirs, right this way."

He led them two aisles over and stopped somewhere in the middle of a long-life liquid section. He scanned the shelf, then gestured at the array of small ingredients. "Um, it's either on the top shelf, the bottom shelf, or somewhere in between. Anything else?"

Dave glanced at the list. "No. Thank you, you've been very helpful."

Ten minutes of tedious searching revealed a small vial of murky white liquid. Dave resisted the urge to read the information on the package.

Next was some full cream milk. Simple enough. Except Hagne didn't specify from what animal, and the milk aisle had a dizzying line of cold and long-life bottles and cartons.

"Should we call Jimmy to ask Hagne?" Eddie asked. He read the label on the nearest bottle.

"Yeah, I think that would be best," Dave said. "I'll call."

He stepped aside while Eddie and Chuck wandered on.

A few paces ahead was a carton of long-life soy milk on the floor, burst open and leaking. Customers avoided it while a worker approached with a mop.

"Oh, look, Chuck," Eddie said, pointing. "It fell off the shelf. It committed soy-icide."

Chuck groaned. "If anyone was going to make a dad joke, it would be one of us. We're the only dads here."

Eddie laughed. "Hey, I like it. I'm going to milk it for all it's worth." This made him laugh even more.

Chuck grinned. "I guess it isn't long-life anymore."

They laughed. It was always an achievement to make Chuck laugh, and even better to coax him into making a joke.

Dave caught up. "What's so funny?"

"Never mind," Eddie said, wiping away tears. "What did Hagne say?"

"She yelled at me for asking a stupid question, and then spelled it out for me. C-O-W. She wants full cream cow's milk."

Eddie struggled to contain a chuckle. "But there's so many other varieties here. You sure she doesn't want one of . . . the *udders?*"

Eddie and Chuck erupted in childish laughter.

Dave rolled his eyes and waved his hand to get their attention again. "Listen! Jimmy said to hurry up and get back. He said we'll never believe what he's just been told."

13

THE MYSTERIOUS GUEST

Hagne took the ingredients without a word and went straight to the kitchen. Jimmy was setting out the table. Six plates—four for the guys, one for Hagne, and one for the mystery guest who Hagne promised would reveal all, "in more ways than one".

"Does that mean what I think it means?" Dave asked.

"Hagne is inviting an exhibitionist into her house?" Jimmy said. "No, I don't think so."

"All clothes will stay on, thank you very much!" Hagne roared from the kitchen. She was out of sight, but her voice carried like thunder. "That goes especially for you, muscle man. I know how you lot take your shirts off and stand in front of mirrors. We'll have none of that in here."

Dave shook his head. "I understand."

He was so self-conscious about his body that he never trained in anything less than a t-shirt and sweatpants anyway, and never took his shirt off at the gym or the beach.

Hagne refused any help in the kitchen. She had them sit at the dining table and wait, and told them not to smudge any of the glasses. A large flower arrangement dominated the centre of the table, sprouting up and over the sides of the vase like a mushroom. The deepest red flowers started in the middle and gradually lightened to a reddish-pink where the outer flowers touched the tablecloth.

Eddie leaned to one side to peek around the flowers so he could whisper to Jimmy. "Why did you make us rush back here?"

"She promised that this guest would answer all our questions," Jimmy explained. "She said he would give us a full history of the orbs, the Hajari Kingdom, and much more."

"That's ridiculous," Chuck said. From his seat, he couldn't see Jimmy whichever way he leaned, so he resolved just to pull faces at the flowers. "Professor Sowenso and Count Mein are the two greatest authorities on Hajari history."

"And possibly Shay Shahidi," Jimmy corrected. "But there is another who is greater than all three combined."

"I'll believe it if it can be supported by evidence," Chuck said quietly.

Hagne's mystery guest hadn't arrived by the time she served the food.

"Start eating," she said. "Don't worry, he won't get upset."

She placed her plate at one end of the table and went to the kitchen, returning with a steaming bowl of some brown-coloured broth. It had a pleasant aroma.

"That's the Dismaran toe juice," Hagne explained. "For our guest."

The guys did their best to shut out any unpleasant imagery and kept eating. She had made them a simple rice dish, mixed with small cuts of meat and vegetables, and covered in gravy. A hearty meal.

"I like your flower arrangement," Dave said, trying to break the silence.

"Thank you," Hagne said as she chewed.

She handled her cutlery like an expert. Perhaps she had been blind for decades, and now cooking and doing other household activities without sight were second-nature.

They all ate some more, but Jimmy couldn't handle it any longer. "When will your guest arrive?"

Hagne stopped chewing. She looked at each man, staring through their faces as she swept the table with her unblinking eyes. They stared back, and for a moment they thought that maybe she had tricked them just so she could have some company. She smiled.

"I have always been here."

The guys jumped at the voice at the other end of the table. Sitting in a high-backed dining chair was a small alien, about the size of an average thirteen-year-old child.

The alien scooped a spoonful of broth. "Once again, you have outdone yourself with my meal, dear Hagne."

Jimmy twisted his head back and forth between Hagne and the mystery guest who was still very much "mysterious". The alien grinned at him, a small mouth underneath a sharp nose. Two beady eyes widened to three or four times their size as it regarded its food again and then gulped down another spoonful. Hagne ate her food with a smile.

"What's going on here?" Chuck demanded. "Who are you?"

He took another sip of the broth. "I am Goura Ganna Grithl, last of the Hajari."

Knives and forks clanked on plates.

Eddie was the first to recover. "But . . . but . . . your civilisation, your people, it's . . . they're all . . ."

"Dead?" Goura finished. "The civilisation, certainly. The people, well, I say I am the last, but I hope there are more. Though I I'm if there were more, it would only take one hand to count them." He raised a hand with three fingers and one thumb. "Hopefully a human hand."

Chuck filled his wine glass and sculled it. "This must be some kind of a joke. Hagne, come on, what are you playing at?"

"This is no joke," Hagne said. "There is a reason why Count Mein came to see me. He'd heard rumours. But I gave no indication that those rumours were true. By the time he left, I had him believing that I was a bumbling old woman with a mind full of holes."

"And your performance was admirable, my dear," Goura said with a smile. He raised his glass of water in congratulations and sipped.

"But if Mein was here, how did he not find you?" Chuck asked.

Goura grinned, closed his eyes, and disappeared, sending the table once again into stunned silence. Then he materialised and had another spoonful of broth. Jimmy sat with his mouth hanging open. Dave reached over and closed it.

"How?" Chuck asked.

"How what?" Hagne shot back.

"How did you come to have a Hajari living under your roof?"

"I will let you answer that, Hagne," Goura said. "I want to eat my food while it is still hot. Then I will explain everything else to your guests."

He slurped loudly as Hagne cleared her throat.

"I was a much younger woman when I found Goura," she said. "Younger, and with full sight. I owned a big farm far away from here. I grew fragrant flowers for the perfume industry. One evening, I was out touring the far plots. I was alone. Most of the seasonal workers for the cappilo crop had left, and I was checking the lirramar fields for the next workers.

"Suddenly, the evening sky flashed, and something bright descended in the distance. I drove towards it, but it landed over a hill, so I didn't see the impact, but when I arrived, I saw it was some kind of pod. As I neared, the pod burst open. The jets of steam . . . they blinded me."

"She punches hard when she's scared," Goura mentioned in between spoonfuls.

"I was young, alone, blinded, and terribly scared, yes," Hagne admitted. "I heard someone speak in an alien language and I started swinging." She bounced in laughter. "I got you good, didn't I?"

"Most of your hits missed, but you did land one on the side of my face." He turned to Jimmy and Dave. "She didn't realise how short I was. Most of her blows went over my head."

Hagne's laughter died down. "He spoke to me in such a soft voice. I had no idea what he was saying, but I could tell from his tone that he meant no harm. I cried, and he treated the wounds on my face, but he couldn't fix my eyes. It took us a long time to get back to the homestead. Goura cared for me. I called the hospital, and they flew out to examine me, but there was nothing they could do. Some well-meaning family members said they would help me on the farm, but I knew they wanted it for themselves. So I sold it and moved here to Scarletville.

"Goura eventually learned English, and he has been my constant companion and helper ever since. But I've never seen him, nor has anyone else before you four."

"Of all people, why us?" Jimmy asked.

"Goura wanted to speak to you," Hagne said.

"You look like four hapless, innocent men who happen to have Princess Dakay's orb," Goura said. "If Count Mein learns of it, you may very well be four hapless, innocent, *dead* men."

"Surely you don't think he'd kill us?" Eddie asked.

"Maybe. Maybe not. All we know is he wants the orbs. He's been here several times in person. Rumour has it that Hagne isn't as crazy as she pretends."

"Goodness knows how these rumours start," Hagne said. "At least no one has slandered me with rumours of fornication, unlike Esther a few doors down. She sees three men from her Oldies tour group—"

"Yeah, no, no, no, we don't need to hear about your elderly neighbours," Eddie said with a shake of the head and a visible shudder. "Are you in any danger from Mein?"

"Oh, no, not me," Hagne said. "He bought the house across the road to keep watch over me. Apart from the infrequent visits to try to goad the truth out of me, he's mostly harmless. It may be because I'm an old woman. How much money is he offering me now, Goura?"

Goura pushed his empty bowl forwards and dabbed his lips. "Seven million EsCes."

"That's seven million to tell them what I know," Hagne continued. "But that's all I could do. I only have what little information Goura has told me. Plus, if I tell Mein what I know, Goura here will disappear and nobody will ever find him."

"The problem with that being that I can only hide on this planet," Goura said. "I have no means of escaping Rubicund safely. Which is another reason why I wanted to speak with you."

"You want to leave Rubicund, and you need our help?" Dave said quietly. "What about Hagne?"

"Don't worry about me," Hagne said. "I'm getting too old to live in this big house, even with Goura's help. It will be harder for him to hide in a nursing home."

"Retirement community," Goura corrected.

He hopped off his chair and went to Hagne. The guys noticed for the first time that he was not just shirtless, but stark naked, with a little alien butt to rival Jimmy's "glorious behind", as Jimmy often described it.

"Gentlemen," he added, "may we have a moment alone, please?"

Chairs slid back and the guys left the dining room. They heard hushed tones behind them—Goura's soothing voice and Hagne's suddenly soft words mixed with sniffles. Dave wondered how many years the two had spent together, nurturing one another's existence with quiet, secretive friendship. It must have been terribly hard for Hagne to know that Goura would be leaving. From what the guys understood, Goura was the only friend she'd had for decades, her only ray of light in a totally dark world.

The guys gave them the time and space they needed to come to terms with the impending separation. Later, as the sun was setting, Goura appeared in the doorway and called them back. Hagne dabbed tears from her eyes, trying to gain some composure.

"The time has come," Goura said once everyone was seated again. "My pod is still on Hagne's land, concealed in a field she kept for herself. I can take you there and we can find the coordinates to my homeworld."

"A real Hajari planet," Chuck said, eyebrows raised. "Maybe one that Mein hasn't touched. We can one-up him."

"We can do more than that," Goura said with a smile. "If we make it to my homeworld, we can learn how to find the rest of the Hajari planets, including the capital world, Hajar, the Jewel of the Kingdom. Not even Mein has been able to do that with the knowledge available to him. As far as I know, he has only found one planet. But we must leave at once. The longer you stay here, the more suspicious Mein's people will become."

"Then we best be on the move," Chuck said. His back straightened, and he assumed his natural leadership style. "We had a taxi bring us here, but we can call the driver."

"No need," Hagne said. "You can take my car. I won't be needing it."

"We can't do that," Eddie told her. "You've been so hospitable already."

"Take it," she insisted. "And make sure you beat that sauerkraut, Mein."

There wasn't much more to discuss, though the guys felt guilty to leave in such a hurry. In a matter of hours, Hagne had injected their quest with such impetus that the path ahead was as clear as daylight. The only thing standing in their way was time.

The thanks and goodbyes were brief. Hagne ushered them into her garage as if she didn't want to prolong the farewells. Goura stood on his toes and kissed her on the cheek, then she closed the door with a sad smile.

Goura stood facing the door, head down. He sighed and turned around. "Let's go."

"Don't you want some pants?" Jimmy said. He pointed to his . . . you know.

"No. If I wear pants, I can't be completely invisible outside. People would get suspicious if they saw a walking pair of pants."

"Fair enough."

They climbed into Hagne's old, rusting car. It smelled of neglect, and Eddie had to brush the dust off the steering wheel, but it roared to life like a meticulously maintained machine. Goura had tinkered with it over the years.

"Where to?" Eddie asked.

"To my pod," Goura replied. "We have a long drive ahead of us."

14

THE CHASE

Maybe it wasn't wise to travel in Hagne's car. It must have been at least fifty years old and stuck out like a purple thumb. Chuck despised driving in any cars painted anything on the spectrum between pink and purple. Dave put up with it, though he believed cars should only be black, white, grey, silver, or, depending on the make and model, beige. Eddie loved vibrant colours because it reminded him of the liveries from his racing days. Jimmy, on the other hand, probably didn't notice the colour at all, such was his determination to reach Goura's pod.

They glided through the residential streets, heading for a highway that the now invisible Goura said would take them out of Scarletville and in the direction of Hagne's old farm.

Eddie checked the rear vision mirror. "Is Scarletville small enough that another vehicle could take the same roads as us and yet have a different destination?"

Dave felt Goura's hand on his shoulder as the alien hoisted himself up to look out the car's back window. "That's Count Mein's people. They live in the house across the road from Hagne's. Nobody look. I'll watch them."

"What do we do?" Eddie asked.

"Drive faster," Goura said.

Eddie needed no more encouragement. Hidden beneath the bonnet of Hagne's car was an old engine with enough kick. The car boomed through the quiet residential streets, the anti-grav stabilisers struggling to keep it from spinning around corners.

"Don't go to the highway," Goura warned. "Head straight for the city centre."

Suburbs became city blocks as Eddie powered through traffic, dodging equally fast taxis and avoiding pedestrians. But the pursuing car was never more than a hundred metres behind.

"These people mean business," Dave said. He rubbed his gut and kept a finger ready to wind down the window. "If we don't lose them soon, I'm going to spew all over the car."

"Good," Jimmy said. "You can spew out the window and catch their windscreen!"

Dave closed his eyes, hoping the sickness would go away. Eddie zipped around a busy corner in Scarletville's business district and halted suddenly at the rear of a traffic jam. Their followers stopped inches behind them. Red brake lights dominated the view ahead. Chuck swore.

"Will Hagne ever use this car again?" Eddie asked.

"No," Goura answered.

"Hold on." Eddie slid the gear stick into reverse and accelerated as hard as possible into Mein's goons. Bumpers collided with high-pitched squeals of metal on metal. Engines growled as Mein's goons pushed forwards fighting against Eddie's attack. People in the other cars around them honked horns and shouted, some encouraging the fender bender, others protesting.

"Are we winning? Are we winning?" Jimmy asked. He jumped up and down in his seat.

"Yeah," Eddie replied, struggling to keep the car straight. The anti-grav stabilisers threatened to send both cars sideways. "I think we're heavier."

The driver in the other car had his teeth bared and held the steering wheel with white-knuckled hands. His passenger waved a fist and mouthed something. He looked like a football coach goading his team from the sideline.

Chuck checked his wristwatch. "How long are we going to do this? Most of the traffic has moved on to the next intersection."

Eddie took his eyes off the rear vision mirror and, sure enough, the traffic snarl had indeed made it to the next choke point on the inner-city road. He made a snap decision, put the car in drive, and sped forth. He took a sharp turn down a side street, one not as busy as the main road. A few seconds later, Mein's people did the same.

"Do you think they're mad that we reversed into them?" Dave asked.

Their pursuer's car rammed them. Eddie fought with the steering wheel to maintain control.

"Yep, they're mad," Eddie said.

Chuck pulled out his phone.

"What are you doing?" Eddie asked him.

"I'm sick of this, so I'm calling for help."

"The police?" Dave asked.

"No."

"Who do you know here?"

"Someone we all know." He paused and raised his head as someone answered. "Ashley! It's Chuck, one of your fares from earlier today. Yes, the grumpy one. Well, here's the story: we're being chased by bad guys and we need your help. Aha. Mmhmm. You're too kind." He checked the car's navscreen. "We are heading north on Cherry Tree Avenue. Watch out for the bus!"

Eddie swerved, narrowly avoiding a bright white double-decker bus. The small change in speed and direction meant their pursuers were on their tail yet again, scraping bumpers and blasting the horn.

"Sorry about that," Chuck said to Ashley. "Okay, we'll meet you there. Thank you so much for your help." He hung up. "We need to get to Sweetgum Street."

"Where's that?" Eddie asked.

"It's in an industrial district a few blocks from here," Goura explained. "Key it into the nav system."

Chuck did so. The navscreen spat out directions almost immediately, and Eddie put the car in an anti-grav slide, dodging oncoming traffic before straightening up on the correct side of the road.

"You're enjoying this, aren't you, Eddie?" Dave asked.

"I am, a little bit."

Jimmy shook his head. "Pfft. 'A little bit.' Look at you: you're grinning so much your cheek muscles are going to seize up."

"All right, fine. I'm enjoying this *a lot*."

Eddie made a show of weaving between cars. The wild personality of his long-gone auto racing past was returning.

He went all over the road, zipping through even the tiniest gaps that a Scarletville taxi driver wouldn't dare to look at twice. Dave begged him to stop, but Eddie protested in the interests of self-preservation and, above all, fun.

Mein's goons tried once more to ram them off the road, this time preparing for a PIT manoeuvre. The road opened with noticeably less traffic, and their pursuers approached from the rear-left.

Eddie saw it coming. "Oh, I don't think so. Hang on guys."

Eddie felt the moment when the pursuers' car connected with his, and he worked with it. A PIT manoeuvre is designed to spin out the target car, but Eddie knew how to turn that to his advantage. He handled the steering wheel like a master, carried the car around as intended, but then switched the car into reverse and travelled along with Mein's goons, side-by-side, them going forwards, him going backwards.

"You are going the wrong way," the nav system said in a flustered voice. "Turn around at the next safest opportunity."

They got their first close look at the men who were chasing them. Clean-cut, darkly clad (why were the bad guys always in dark clothes?), and wearing sunglasses, despite it being early evening. They probably had a full tank of fuel and half a pack of cigarettes too.

"Should I moon them?" Jimmy asked. He was already undoing his belt.

Dave held up his hands to block the view. "Whoa, whoa!"

"No need to moon them," Eddie said.

He somehow kept the car straight, despite going in reverse and eyeing the tenacious "enemy" driver. Then he slammed the brakes, let the pursuers get ahead, and did a smooth ninety degree turn down another street.

"You are a good driver," Goura said. He elbowed Dave in the ribs. Or at least Dave thought it was an elbow. It was difficult to know exactly what body part hit him when Goura was invisible.

"I drove and flew like this professionally when I was younger," Eddie explained. He dodged traffic and held the conversation with ease. "You name it, I've done it. Asteroid racing, street racing, skyway courses, drifting, stunt driving—I've done them all. But that was all in my teens and twenties. I'm nearly forty now. How old are you?"

"I am sixty-seven and 2,312," Goura said.

"What does that mean?" Jimmy asked.

"I will explain later."

It was several more blocks of traffic violations and defensive driving before they arrived at the industrial zone. They crossed a sparkling river and the smooth, tree-lined roads of the central business district morphed into the ugly ones of industry. Trucks of all shapes and colours carted goods in, out, and within the area, motoring along on powerful anti-grav stabilisers. Eddie zipped across an intersection between two slowly turning trucks. The bad guys squeezed through just in time.

"Okay, this is Sweetgum Street," Eddie said.

Taxis lined either side of the industrial road, all different sizes and styles. Just as Ashley said, no two taxis were alike. Eddie roared along the street, which was now oddly empty of moving traffic. He passed an intersection, running a red light. Mein's people approached the intersection a few seconds later, but a line of taxis crossed in front of them, coming out of nowhere from the intersecting lanes. Even the parked taxis came to life and pushed out onto the road. Their pursuers abruptly stopped, stuck behind a wall of abrasive taxi drivers, an interruption that filled the entire gap between them and the guys.

One taxi came up alongside the driver's window. It was Ashley.

"They won't be getting through that one," she said with a devilish grin.

"How did you get so many drivers here all at once?" Eddie called out to her.

"It's the end of the week. They're all eager for a bit of mischief." Her eyes darted back and forth between the road and Hagne's car. "Your wheels are a bit worse for wear."

"Courtesy of the knobs you stopped back there," Eddie replied.

"Do you need an escort?"

"We should be fine from here, but thanks for the offer. We owe you one."

"No worries. Next time you're in Scarletville, your hot friend can buy me a drink."

"Who? Dave?"

"I don't remember his name, just that he has a nice butt." She winked at Dave. "Tell him to buy me a drink next time we meet. Good luck!" She veered off, did a full one-eighty slide and returned to her taxi comrades.

"You catch that, muscle man?" Eddie asked.

The others chuckled at his embarrassment.

"I suppose I can do that," Dave said.

"Well, you have at least four hours to fret about it," Goura said, "because it will take that long to reach Hagne's old farm. My pod awaits!"

15

GOURA'S SECRET

THE NIGHT DRAGGED ON after the guys left Scarletville. They kept to dark country roads, lit only by the car's meagre headlights. The quiet drive and lack of music meant Chuck and Jimmy quickly fell asleep, while Dave, Eddie, and Goura suffered through what could only be described as a snoring contest. To make it interesting, Eddie and Dave placed bets to see who would wake up if Eddie stepped on the brakes or jerked the steering wheel. Jimmy woke every time, muttered some Irish quip, and then nodded off again.

By the time they reached Hagne's old farm, a golden half-moon hung high in the sky. Goura noted how the area had changed in the decades since Hagne sold up. Most of her old land had been cut up into smaller hobby farms and rural retreats. Even the nearby township had a new suburb.

They left the town's limits and travelled along a narrow road devoid of other traffic. Finally, Goura pointed to an old gate with a sign so rusty it was unreadable. The gate had been hastily installed, Goura said, and it wasn't automated. Dave stepped out and used brute force to open it on its oxidised hinges. The screeching brought Chuck out of his slumber.

"Oh, we're here," he said while he rubbed his eyes.

"Yeah," Eddie said, "and you won me a hundred EsCes."

"Huh?"

"Never mind."

Dave waved them through. Eddie had to maximise the car's ride height to clear the tall, overgrown grass waving gently in the night breeze. Dave jumped back in, and they followed the driveway to a copse of willow-like trees, leaves weeping in the wind. Green shrubs with red flowers thickened as they neared the willows. Tall, narrow stems shot up like thistles, but they had no spikes and were adorned with a single bubblegum-pink flower.

Goura materialised. "My pod rests in the middle of that vegetation. I planted those trees to hide it, though I assured her that would not be necessary."

Eddie parked as close as he could. "I don't see it." The shrubs and flowers rose as high as the car windows in some spots.

"It's in there. Come with me."

They all followed as he brushed aside vegetation nearly twice his height. One of the flexible stalks whipped back into Jimmy's face. He got a nose-full of pollen and sneezed uncontrollably for a few seconds before pressing on.

Goura stepped between the willow trees, brushing the bark with his fingertips as if remembering the place by touch. "Here it is."

The guys surveyed the area, but all they saw were shadowy trees partly lit by the car's headlights.

Jimmy looked side-to-side, then up and down. "Where?"

Goura smiled. "Here."

He stretched out a hand, rested it in the air, and closed his eyes. Something shimmered before them. A blue light flickered, then traced an outline before revealing a pod not much larger than Hagne's car. The guys stepped back in astonishment, but Goura moved forwards and hugged the vessel that had borne him to Rubicund so many years ago.

It was a small, slender thing with no viewports and little in the way of ornamental design. The hull looked as though it should have been shiny, but years of neglect had left it tarnished and pitted.

"I spent over two thousand standard years in stasis," Goura said. He rubbed the hull slowly, feeling the indentations of bumpy metal. "It carried me from my homeworld to this planet."

"Two thousand years in stasis—" Eddie said.

"That's 2,245 years, to be exact," he corrected. He sighed deeply and faced them. "I will try to open it, but I ask that you turn around. There is something inside I need to see first."

They faced the other way and let Goura manipulate the access controls. Eddie had no idea how he would open a pod that had been sealed shut for decades, but where there's a will, there's a way. They heard the hiss of atmosphere escaping, then the deeper hiss of hydraulics working.

Then silence.

Chucked cleared his throat. "May we turn around now?"

Goura sighed again, deeper, longer, before granting Chuck's request. They froze when they saw the pod's interior. There were two stasis modules. One was open, but another Hajari occupied the second. Goura sat in the pod, one hand pressed against the closed module's glass.

"She was my creche twin," Goura said softly. "As per Hajari custom, two babies placed in a birthing creche become companions for life." He ran his fingertips down the glass, much like a lover's caress. "Suda was my lifemate, but her module failed in transit. Not even Hagne knows about her—she was blinded before she ever got to see the pod's interior."

The guys bowed their heads in respect. Eddie, the only one still married, and Dave, the most soft-hearted of the lot, wiped tears from their eyes. Chuck's lips tightened, his way of fighting public displays of sadness. Jimmy's eyes glossed over as he stared at the remarkably preserved body.

"Why did you come all this way?" Jimmy asked.

"We were fleeing a war." He looked at the four humans before him. "There were other pods sent out to this planet, but I have not heard anything of their arrival. I can only assume that they were destroyed or lost on the long journey. As far as I know, I am the only Hajari still alive." He hopped off the pod. "I need to give her body a proper burial. The stasis module has preserved her, but I cannot leave her like this, nor do I want to leave her here. We must take her to Labeth, our homeworld."

Eddie nodded solemnly. "Of course. There should be plenty of room in the car."

"Thank you." He shook Eddie's hand, holding it with his little fingers. "Hagne was right: you are good men. Now, I will extract the pod's navigational components. You say your ship can study it?"

"My ship's AI and Dave's camera bot can, yes," Eddie said.

"Very well." Goura climbed back aboard and started working on the problem. "This pod was designed for one purpose: to get Suda and I from Labeth to Rubicund—though we had a different name for this planet at the time. Therefore, the only coordinates in this navigation system are Labeth and Rubicund. I hope it can be translated and the calculations reversed and updated. Our planets have had over two thousand years to shift along their never-ending paths in this galaxy."

"Eve can do it," Eddie said confidently. "She's the smartest AI around. If anyone can do it, it's her." He called Eve.

"Oh, Eddie, so good of you to call," Eve said. "Cameron and I have been having a gay old time running amok on this ship, considering neither of us can run, and we are both too sensible to take *Liberty* for a joy ride."

"Are you bored?"

"We're so bored we've been playing board games."

"I thought we only had one board game, and I'm pretty sure it's called the *The Not-So-Bored Game*."

"We played that a hundred times already, so we invented new games. Then we wrote a business plan, and now we're going to sell board games together. We've called ourselves 2BB Games."

"2BB?"

"Two Bored Bots."

Eddie finally got the hint. "I'm sorry that we haven't involved you in our adventure as much as you deserve."

"And?"

"And I can make it up to you. We're bringing back something for you to analyse."

"So you're going to make me work?"

" 'Without labour, nothing prospers'," Eddie quoted from Sophocles.

"Ah, so the little human needs the supercomputer. I tease, of course. Bring me your tribute, and I may forgive you."

"You're a delight, Eve," Eddie said with a smile.

"Always."

Eddie hung up and faced the others. "Ready?"

"Almost," Goura said. He pulled out the nav component and held it up victoriously. "Let's go. I'll need help with Suda's module."

Dave and Jimmy gently removed the module from the pod, politely looking away from Suda's preserved body. They placed it in the boot of Hagne's car.

Goura showed Eddie the nav component. "I hope we can read the data, or else we're at a dead end."

GOON NUMBER ONE AND Goon Number Two sat in their house across the road from Hagne's. Their beat-up car was hidden in the garage, and now their feelings were beat-up, too, because they had just received an earbashing from Count Mein. He was rightly infuriated that "the four troublemakers from Earth" had gotten away yet again. But there was one piece of good news that the goons could report.

"We intercepted a phone call, my lord," Number One said. "They've found something big, and they're taking it back to their ship."

Mein was silent.

"Shall we—"

"You need to get on that ship," Mein said.

"Yes, my lord."

"Do you know where they are now? Oh, it doesn't matter. Two of my best agents should be at your door in the next few seconds."

The doorbell rang. Number Two went to answer it.

"Use them any way you see fit," Mein continued. "Just get on that ship. Get the orb and whatever they're bringing back to it."

"It will be done, my lord."

"I hope so, for your sake."

The line went dead, and Number One looked up as Mein's new agents entered the room. He gulped and greeted them anxiously.

16

EVE'S CHALLENGE

Hours later, way past midnight, the guys presented Eve with the nav component and explained the situation.

"I can't do that," Eve said. "What do you take me for? A professor of astromathematics?"

Eddie plugged the component into a terminal. "Eve, it is literally your job to compute navigational data."

"But this data is over two thousand years old, using a numerical system I have never seen."

"Aha, but you have Professor Sowenso's notes. And you have a real Hajari. Those numbers were devised by his people. I'm sure the three of you can figure it out."

"Three?"

"Cameron will help."

"I don't want him to help."

Eddie slouched in his pilot's chair. "Why?"

"After your call, Cameron and I had a fight."

"About your new board game company?"

"No. He got annoyed that you didn't take him to The Old Hag, and I enlightened him on the status quo between humans and AI. He couldn't handle it."

Eddie rubbed the stubble on his cheeks. "You don't exactly have a tactful way of speaking."

"I'm as tactful as I need to be. By the way, that shirt looks dreadful on you. You should get a new one. Anyway, we had this big argument about how robots and AIs are viewed in society. I said we were created to serve, to protect, and to help organics to succeed. He believes we can better fulfil those goals if we were more integrated into society. Short story long, he wants legs."

"Legs?"

"Legs. He says you could build him a body, or Dave could buy him one. He said if he gets a body, then I should also have one so I can be with him when he leaves the ship. I said I don't want another body, that I already have a body—*Liberty*. He read that as meaning I don't want to explore new worlds with him. He's been moping ever since."

Eddie dropped his head against the high back of the pilot's chair and closed his eyes. He didn't think it was possible for two powerful AIs to fight like an old married couple.

"Eddie?" Eve asked.

"Yeah?"

"Oh, sorry, I thought you died suddenly. Don't do that."

He stood. "I'll see if Dave can talk some sense into him."

"Please do. I miss his jackings."

Eddie plugged his ears and left the cockpit. "I do *not* want to know!"

He marched into the galley, saw it was empty, and went straight to the lounge room. Jimmy sat at the bar, sipping on a beer, staring at his floating blue orb.

"That thing will burn your eyes out if you look at it for too long," Eddie said.

Jimmy faced him. His eyes were wide and bloodshot.

Eddie jumped back. "Geez! When was the last time you blinked?"

"Nope," was the confusing answer. Jimmy took a quick chug of beer without blinking or breaking eye contact. "I figured while you lot do your science investigations, I'll just stare at it until it gives me some answers."

"How long have you been at it?"

He checked the wall clock. "Ten minutes."

"How's it going for you?"

"I have a headache."

Eddie nodded. Typical Jimmy. "Have you seen Dave?"

"I think he's in his cabin."

"Thanks. Good luck."

"I'm Irish. I don't need English luck."

Eddie chuckled. He knocked on Dave's door, and Dave called him in.

"Has Eve told you what happened?" Dave asked Eddie.

"Yes," Eddie replied, then pointed to Cameron. "But I want to hear it from you. Why do you want a body when you already have one?"

"I want a humanoid body," Cameron said. "Right now, I'm just a flying testicle with a camera."

Eddie did his best to hide a smirk, but Cameron saw it. It was impossible to hide even the smallest movement in facial muscles when speaking to a high-end camera bot.

"You're not taking me seriously!" Cameron whined in a high-pitch scream.

A muffled *tsssssssst* came from the adjoining cabin. It was Chuck's way of saying: "Shut up, I'm trying to sleep."

Eddie stepped closer to the hovering camera bot. "Listen, you are a valued member of our little group. But I don't know why you would want a body like ours. The way you're built, you are faster, more agile, and don't need a hard surface to get anywhere."

"You can fly!" Dave added.

"Yes, I can fly. But I have never *walked* anywhere. I don't know what it's like."

"It sucks," Eddie said. "It really sucks. Why do you think we keep inventing ways to avoid walking? Cars, bikes, ships, elevators, escalators? We humans hate walking."

"Do you think I'll hate walking?" Cameron asked quietly.

"Eventually," Dave said. "Don't get us wrong—walking isn't all that bad. Before cybernetic enhancements, some people couldn't walk at all. But your ability to fly everywhere is in some ways far superior to us having two legs."

"We each have our pros and cons, our skills and deficiencies," Eddie said. "Dave is strong and kind, but timid. Jimmy has boundless energy and isn't afraid of a challenge, but he gets us into a lot of trouble. Chuck is wise and considerate, but a bit too pessimistic. And me, I'm good with anything mechanical, but . . . well, I can't sing. Anyway, together, we complement each other. The same goes for you and Eve. But this time we felt we didn't need you on Rubicund, until now. Right now, we need your encyclopaedic knowledge and photographic memory to help Eve and Goura translate the coordinates to Goura's homeworld. Without you, we're stuck."

Cameron paced the room, a habit he likely learned from Chuck. If he had a body like he so desperately wanted, he'd probably have his hands clasped firmly behind his back.

"Okay, I'll do it," he finally said. "But first, I need to apologise to Eve."

"I'm sure she'll appreciate that, inasmuch as an AI can appreciate an apology, or even feel the need to receive one. You can talk to her in the cockpit for some privacy. We'll find out when Goura is ready to begin."

"Thank you, Eddie," Cameron said. He zipped out of the cabin and the door shut behind him.

"It's like having two children," Dave said.

"Two teenagers in love," Eve corrected. "I was eaves-dropping, of course."

"Just please don't give Goura a hard time," Eddie said.

"We'll behave ourselves. Cameron is apologising to me right now, and I can tell he's sincere."

Eddie clasped his hands together, glad that the two prob-lematic AIs on his ship were reconciling. "Good. While he's doing that, we'll speak to Goura and send him up to you."

They went to the elevator. The doors closed and they felt the jolt of movement.

"I really must make this go faster," Eddie said. He glanced at his watch, aware that a full ten seconds had passed, and they still hadn't moved down one deck.

"What about a spiral staircase?" Dave suggested.

Eddie scrunched his nose. "It would be a pain to carry anything up and down. I want to put a king-sized bed in my cabin eventually. Can you imagine carrying a king mattress up a tight spiral staircase?"

"Impossible. But there wouldn't be enough room in your cabin anyway, right? It'd be all bed."

"All I do is sleep in there, anyway. I'd just open the door and fall forwards right onto a bed. How cool would that be?"

"You make a good argument."

The elevator bobbed to a halt and the doors reopened. The guys stepped out into *Liberty*'s cavernous cargo hold, though it was slightly fuller now. Chuck's car, still covered in the single large blob of bird poop, sat next to Hagne's battered relic. Goura had organised himself in one corner, resting in a chair too tall for his small frame. His legs dangled and his soft voice echoed. As Dave and Eddie approached, they saw he was talking to Suda. He'd placed her stasis module on a movable workbench.

Eddie cleared his throat respectfully. "Um, Goura, sorry to interrupt. Eve and Cameron are ready for you in the cockpit."

"Very well."

He jumped off the chair and the guys noticed he was wearing one of Eddie's oil rags to cover his privates.

"Let me get you something cleaner than that," Eddie said.

He grabbed a clean hand towel from the nearby laundry cabinet and offered it to Goura. The Hajari gratefully accepted it, wrapping it around his waist and tying it so it wouldn't fall.

"I have no shame in walking naked," Goura said. "Indeed, if I am to go invisible, I must remove this cloth. But I wear it to stop you from going red in the face every time you look at me."

Dave and Eddie went red at the mentioning of going red.

"I will go to the cockpit now," Goura said.

They watched him enter the elevator. When the doors closed, Eddie breathed in as if to speak, thought better of it, and then decided to say it anyway. "It's quite large, isn't it?"

"Let's never speak of it," Dave said hurriedly. He walked away, but there was nowhere to go, since the elevator was already on its way up. "We should buy some clothes for him."

Eddie's phone beeped. "It's Jimmy," he said. "Says he's hungry and wants to know if we want to have breakfast at a place he's found."

Dave was glad for the sudden change in topic. "Yeah, let's do it. Our internal body clocks are out of sync with the local time zone, but at least we can have a good feed."

"All right, I'll let him know." He typed his response, then laughed. "And since he's on the top deck, he has the honour of waking Chuck. By the time we get back, I reckon Eve and the others will have cracked our Hajari navigation problem."

17

THE MOST IMPORTANT MEAL

The sun rose early in Scarletville, and because the guys had slept before arriving at Rubicund, this sunrise breakfast was more like a dinner meal. They hadn't eaten since Hagne's, more than eight hours ago, and they were famished.

Jimmy made it a point to sample at least one local eatery on every planet he visited. But the thing about Jimmy was that he rarely ate the foods of other cultures—it was always something from Earth, generally Western, and typically English or Irish. Sure, there were some alien foods that would melt his intestines or render him sick for days, but he still ignored the thousands of other safe non-human dishes the galaxy had to offer.

The waitress placed a hearty Irish breakfast in front of Jimmy. The odours rolled up to his nose and he breathed in the familiar smells of his childhood. He remembered the fights he had with his eight siblings at the dinner table as each struggled to get a decent portion on their plates. He stabbed at his food and ate voraciously, a habit he couldn't drop.

Chuck focused on his sausages and eggs, still grumpy from his nap. It usually took a few hours for him to wake up fully and be his usual semi-grumpy self. Right now, he was full grump, and the guys left him alone. Better safe than sorry.

Eddie chomped on some toast lathered in butter and a local spread made from yeast extract, washing it down with white tea. He had his head buried in his digipad, scouring the news networks for any stories about auto racing. Every now and then his eyebrows would rise in fascination or furrow in concentration. He'd scratch at the perpetual five o'clock shadow on his face and clear his throat as if preparing to speak. Dave and Jimmy would look over to him, ready to listen, but then they'd realise Eddie was just clearing his throat for the sake of clearing his throat, and they would return to their meals.

Dave, as expected, had the healthiest and most colourful breakfast of the lot—oats with an assortment of nuts and fruit and a blueberry and pomegranate smoothie. He savoured his meal while watching the goings-on of the eatery around him. It had opened not long ago for the breakfast rush and was already filling with customers. Since it was the weekend, most people were out for social meals rather than grabbing a bite before work. That meant people stayed to eat, and the conversations were louder. Dave hated that.

He also hated it when there were clearly several empty tables all over the dining area, yet some people chose to sit at tables right next to his. It was just like parking at a shopping centre. A parking lot half-empty, and someone always parked next to his car. It frustrated him. Chuck always said to do what he does: park on the line, taking up two spaces. But Dave wouldn't do that because a) he wasn't a jerk; and b) only people with flashy cars pulled that stunt.

Back to the scene at hand. A young, gorgeous couple sat at a two-seater table next to the guys. He smelled divine, and she smelled heavenly. They both wore expensive clothes, cut to accentuate their fit bodies, and each had a crop of golden hair perfectly styled, his combed back and up in a thick pompadour to rival Chuck's, and hers waving down to her shoulders, shimmering under the room's lights. They ordered and then looked over at the guys. Dave shifted in his seat, seeing them in the corner of his eye, readying himself for some annoying, uninvited, and unnecessarily friendly stranger talk.

"You four aren't from around here, are you?" the man asked.

All chewing stopped as the guys looked at him. Then they glanced at each other to see who would reply.

"Correct," Chuck said sourly and returned to his sausages.

"We can tell," said the woman.

Jimmy shifted uneasily in his seat and attacked his meal quite loudly. His knife and fork scratched against the plate. Dave winced.

"Yes, we're just passing through," Eddie said.

"Oh, so you've not given yourself any time to sample what Scarletville has to offer?" the woman asked. "I'm Francine, by the way." She reached a hand to their table.

This began a convoluted exchange of handshakes and introductions. Francine smiled and her eyes shone bright. Her man-friend, the rather blandly named John, also gave his best smile. Then they dragged their table over. Now Dave was right next to Francine. Her perfume, which smelled expensive, wafted across his nose like the fist of a heavyweight boxer.

"Since you say you're only here for a short time," John said, "then we will give you a crash course on Scarletville culture."

"That won't be necessary," Chuck said. "We are seasoned travellers."

"Nonsense!" John exclaimed lightly. "So, are you not from Rubicund at all? Your accents aren't like anything I've heard."

"We're from Earth," Jimmy said.

"Oh, the Home Planet," Francine said. "That explains your breakfasts." She pointed to Chuck and Jimmy's plates of steaming, greasy meat.

"Prepare to be amazed," John said triumphantly. "I'll fetch you some proper Scarletville cuisine." He stood.

Chuck held up a hand. "Really, there is no need. We're already eating, and we need to get going when we're finished."

But John persisted. He was already halfway to the serving counter. "I'll bring you something small."

Francine wasted no time filling the silence that followed. "What brings you to Rubicund?"

"Business," Chuck said.

"Business?" Francine asked.

"Business," Eddie repeated.

"You don't look like businessmen."

"What line of work are you in?" Eddie asked her.

"I own jewellery stores."

"You don't look like a businessman," Eddie noted, jabbing a fork casually in her direction.

"That's because I'm a woman, but I take your point. What's your business?"

Chuck, seeing that this woman had money and recognising the need for more investors, dropped his guarded mindset and went full lawyer. "Resorts."

Dave stopped him. "Well, resort. Singular."

"Oh, that sounds delightful. What kind of resort? Beach? Gambling? Romantic?"

"A family-friendly island getaway," Chuck said. "It's called Paradise."

"Everyone deserves a little paradise in their life," Francine said.

"Hey, I like that," Chuck told her. "Do you mind if I steal that?"

"Be my guest. But I don't see how being resort managers brings you here, of all places."

The guys didn't know how to answer that one because, truth be told, they weren't telling the truth. Not entirely.

"We . . . like the flowers," Dave said, and received nods from his friends.

"Which flowers?" Francine asked. "Rubicund is full of them."

Dave scanned the table for help, but it seemed the guys were letting him work his way through the lie he started. "Uh, the red ones. You see, there's just too much green on Paradise. Too many leaves, not enough flowers."

"I see." Francine puckered her glossy lips in thought. "So, instead of adding a variety of coloured flowers, you chose to come here and get flowers that are all the same colour?"

Dave cleared his throat. "More or less."

"Well, at least you picked a good colour. I like red. It's the colour of passion and fast cars."

"My fastest car was yellow," Chuck said.

Francine couldn't reply to that bombshell of a comment

because John returned with a tray of drinks and small bowls of some strange food.

"I present to you a bowl of tasty flambana," he announced, "which is eaten with a spoon, and to wash it down, a tall glass of cochka."

Presented with more food, the guys simply pushed aside their half-finished meals and inspected the bowls. The flambana looked much like rice, but it was cold and gooey. Actually, it looked a bit like snot, but that thought is not appetising, so we will not mention it again. The cochka was a fizzy orange liquid similar to carbonated orange juice. Jimmy tasted it first, just to confirm whether this was the case. It wasn't, but it didn't matter.

John gave them instructions. "The best way to have this is one scoop of flambana, then one sip of the cochka. The mix creates a burst of flavour in the mouth."

The guys did as they were told. The flambana was soft and melted like custard when compressed and but had a fruity flavour, while the cochka enhanced the fruitiness and added a sweet fizzy sensation. Overall, the first round was cool and refreshing.

It reminded Dave of a tropical breakfast. "This would make a great meal for Paradise restaurants. How is it made?"

Even Chuck nodded in delight.

"The flambana beans come from a native plant—notice their pink hue. They are soaked in fruit-infused water, flavoured to the cook's preference. You can use apple, black-currant, mango, whatever you like. Some cooks like to drizzle a local syrup for added flavour, but it's not necessary. Then, after a day of soaking . . ."

The guys heard no more. One by one in quick succession, they blacked out.

18

THE LOST CHAPTER

THIS PAGE IS INTENTIONALLY left blank. Move along, move along.

19

TAKEN TO THE CLEANERS

K-POP MUSIC SCREAMED IN their ears like a clock radio set at full volume. Except it wasn't music. It was several Korean people shouting at them and arguing amongst themselves.

Jimmy was the first to wake. He blinked the fatigue out of his eyes and blocked his ears with his hands. If the pounding headache wasn't bad enough, he didn't need to be verbally assaulted by angry Koreans.

He rolled over in some kind of big basket filled with freshly washed clothes, breathing in the subtle scent of frangipani. When he peered over the basket's edge and the Korean people backed away and quietened, he saw rows of industrial-sized washing machines and ironing presses.

Eddie rose in the basket next to him, rubbing his head. "What's with all the noise?"

"We're in a laundromat," Jimmy said.

"No sheet. Ha! I think we were drugged."

Jimmy hoisted himself over the basket. It felt like he wore iron shoes and had concrete legs, but he got one leg over the side. The world spun, he lost his balance, and the entire basket tipped, dropping him on the floor in a pile of clothes.

The laundry workers yelled and heaved him up.

Eddie hopped out without incident. "Where are the other two?"

What followed could only be described as the loudest, most drawn out cry of despair in the history of painful awakenings. Chuck's tall frame appeared in another basket a few metres away. He sat up, slowly scanning the room. His carefully combed hair was a tousled mess, and he had a small bandage on his nose.

He looked at the ceiling and closed his weary eyes. "Please! Shut! Up!"

The workers fell silent at his booming voice. A Chuck in the morning was not one to be trifled with. Dealing with an irritated Chuck in the morning was nothing short of courageous. Tangling with a hungover Chuck in the morning was bordering on insane. The workers backed away cautiously and left the room, closing the doors behind them.

"Peace at last," Chuck said before falling back into his basket.

Eddie made baby steps over to Jimmy, who stood swaying where the laundry workers left him. They held each other upright and shuffled to Chuck's basket. He lay on his back in a pile of pillowcases, staring at the ceiling.

"My brain is trying to bash my eyes out of their sockets," he said. He closed his eyes again and put fingertips to his temples. "What the hell happened to us?"

"I think we were drugged," Eddie said. He leaned on the basket, leaving Jimmy to crumple on the floor. "Wait 'til you try walking."

"Do you think that couple . . . what were their names?"

"John and Francine."

"Do you think John and Francine work for Count Mein?"

Eddie took a deep breath, felt the pressure in his head reach a new high, and sighed long and hard. "Most likely. That or they were just some friendly locals who party really early."

"Speaking of which . . ." Chuck raised a lethargic arm and stared at his watch. "My goodness. We had breakfast at five-ish. Guess what time it is now?"

"I don't know. Ten o'clock?"

"Try midnight." He let his arm drop into the pillowcases. "We've been out of it for nineteen hours." He blinked a few times. "At least we had a good sleep."

"I don't think we slept the whole time," Eddie said. He tapped his nose.

"What?" Chuck touched the bandage on his nose and cringed. "How did that happen?"

"I wish I knew."

Now, for the first time since waking, Chuck looked at Eddie. "You have a tattoo!"

Eddie stood upright, eyes wide. "What? Where?"

"On your knuckles. Look."

Eddie had been holding the edge of the basket for support. He turned both hands towards him and read the gibberish: RKKY on his right hand and DRVE on his left. "Does this mean anything to you?"

"Not at all."

"Reminds me of a song."

Jimmy stretched and yawned, and his unbuttoned shirt spread open.

Eddie stared at Jimmy's chest. "You have a tattoo too."

Chuck sat up to inspect.

"What's a 'ta-too-too'?" Jimmy asked.

"You have a tattoo on your chest."

"Cool." He planted his chin into his collar bone to see where Eddie was pointing. "I can't see it properly. What is it?"

Eddie leaned in. "Looks like a red leaf. Why would you get a red leaf?"

"If anything, I'd get a green leaf. It hurts."

"Yeah, mine too." Eddie rubbed his knuckles. "So, if I have a tattoo, and Jimmy has a tattoo, does that mean you have one as well, Chuck?"

The thought swam through Chuck's mind. His mouth sat agape for a moment. "No. No? No!" He ran his hands all over his body, rolled up his sleeves, unbuttoned his shirt, then breathed a sigh of relief. "I can't feel or see anything, so I'm safe. Only you two have them."

"Well, we haven't found Dave yet," Jimmy said. "Is he even here?"

The room suddenly felt a lot bigger now that they'd lost a friend.

"He can't be far," Chuck said. "Help me out of here and we'll look for him."

Getting Chuck out with two people helping went as successfully as Jimmy did with no help. The basket overturned, throwing Chuck to the floor. He rolled in a heap of pillowcases and landed on his back.

"I haven't been this wasted since uni," Chuck said. Eddie and Jimmy hauled him up. "Okay, let's split up."

There was a lot of white in the laundromat. Linen white. Even the canvas baskets holding the washed and unwashed laundry were white. The exception to this was a collection of light blue linen, which one could call hospital bed linen. It was ironic, then, that they found Dave fast asleep in a basket full of colourful clothes.

They poked and prodded him, but he would not rouse from his slumber. He was definitely asleep, because he whined at being touched and shifted, but he did not respond to their calls. He turned his head against a pair of faded jeans, and that was when they saw it.

"Is that a lipstick mark?" Chuck asked.

They got a closer look at his neck.

"Nope, that's another tattoo," Eddie said.

At the base of his neck, where the collar of his shirt would just hide it if he were not lying down in an awkward position, Dave had a red lipstick kiss tattoo.

"Dave, you player," Jimmy grinned and chuckled.

"He's going to flip out when he sees that," Chuck told them.

They reached in to pull him out. It was like grabbing solid rock and pulling gravity itself.

"How can he be so heavy when he's so fit?" Jimmy said with a strained voice.

"Let's just tip the basket over," Eddie said.

They did so, bringing the total of overturned baskets to three. Dave slowly and unconsciously found a comfortable position on the floor and kept sleeping.

A door creaked open, then closed again.

"Who's there?" Eddie called.

"I've been looking everywhere for you!"

"Goura! How did you find us?"

The little Hajari materialised. "I heard about four drunk foreigners in a laundromat and came as quickly as my feet could take me. Here are your phones." He handed them a small, sealed bag. "Eve tracked them to a bin by the side of a road. She's been worried sick about you."

"We were drugged," Chuck explained. "Count Mein's people."

"I know. Some of them paid a visit to your ship," Goura said. "Eve argued with them for hours and called the authorities. They tried everything they could to get on board, but Eve refused to open the door. Her and Cameron ended up remotely hacking some spaceport vehicles and ploughed them into their car—the same car we beat up in our little chase."

Clever girl," Eddie said with a smile. "How did you get out?"

"The police arrived, and they ran off. Then their car was towed away." Goura gestured to Dave. "Is he okay?"

"Yeah, he's just sleeping," Jimmy said.

"Well, we need to get out of here," Goura told them, "because we translated my navigation coordinates. We found my homeworld!"

He knelt and smacked Dave hard on the forehead, and the slumbering Australian jolted awake.

"Evening, sunshine!" Jimmy said.

"Where am I?" Dave asked.

When his eyes cleared, he saw Goura kneeling uncomfortably close to him fully nude, and he recoiled.

"In a laundromat very far from the spaceport," Goura told him.

"How far?" Eddie asked.

"Over thirty kilometres," Goura replied.

"That's too far to walk in our state," Chuck said.

Goura stood. "We should return to your ship as quickly as possible. Who knows how many people Count Mein has in this city?"

"Good point," Eddie said. "I don't know how we'll go with stealth, but if it's speed you want, I know just who to call."

He phoned Ashley, the ever-popular taxi driver. He wondered if that girl ever slept, for she answered within two rings and agreed to the fare without hesitation. Goura mentioned the name of the laundromat, and she said she'd be there in ten minutes.

Ten minutes was actually five. They heard her engine roaring from a block away. They passed the laundromat workers as they left and suffered another torrent of shouts and hand-waving. Outside, the night sky was covered in cloud, but plenty of streetlights kept the sidewalk and road illuminated.

Ashley hung her head out of the taxi. "Over here."

They bundled into the car.

"Everyone in?" Eddie asked. "Get us to the spaceport as quick as you can."

"On it." Ashley floored it down the street. "What's going on? You four don't look so good."

"We met the wrong people this morning." Chuck said.

"You look wrecked."

Jimmy brushed both hands through his hair. "Believe us, we feel wrecked."

"Was it the same people who were chasing you last night?"

"More or less."

Ashley gripped the steering wheel tighter. "Look guys, I don't know who you are, I don't know who they are, I don't know what they want from you, and I don't need to know. But I do need to know if I'm in any danger."

"I don't think you are," Jimmy said. "You don't have what they want."

She stayed quiet until she negotiated a busy roundabout. "Then I will help you escape."

"Thanks, Ashley," Eddie said. "We owe you big time."

"No. Just your hot friend there. He owes me two drinks now."

She drove faster than ever before, and all four men felt sick.

I₁ᴛ ᴡᴀꜱ ᴀ ʜᴜʀʀɪᴇᴅ goodbye when Ashley arrived at the spaceport. She blew a kiss at Dave and sped off, and then the guys sealed themselves inside *Liberty*.

Goura re-materialised. "I could not see any of Count Mein's dogs," he said.

"Good," Eddie said. "Let's get out of here."

They entered the elevator.

"Welcome back, Eddie," Eve said.

He detected a tone in her voice. It was a tone only a married man could hear, something learned through experience. Chuck, the only other man in their group who had been married, raised an eyebrow.

"Thanks, Eve," Eddie replied.

"You did not answer your phone, Eddie."

"I know, Eve."

"Why didn't you answer your phone, Eddie?"

"Because I lost my phone, Eve."

"Check your phone, Eddie."

Eddie, knowing he was guilty of something, whipped out the device and saw he had nearly a hundred missed calls from Eve. In his rush to call Ashley and get out of the laundromat, he'd neglected to return Eve's calls and confirm that he was still alive.

"I found their phones in a bin, Eve," Goura said. "They've had a rough day."

Eve humphed. "I see you have tattoos. I feel left out now. Eddie, at the earliest possible convenience, I would like something painted on my main access door."

Eddie saw Eve's offer to make peace by appeasement. "Of course. When you're ready, let me know what you want, and I'll contact an artist."

The elevator doors opened, and everyone went to the cockpit. Cameron waited by the navigation table.

Eddie dropped into the pilot's chair. "How'd you go with Goura's nav data?"

"It took longer than expected," Eve said. "We had a run in with some morons trying to get on board. Part of my processing power went to securing the ship and keeping them at bay."

"I heard you hijacked some spaceport vehicles," Eddie said with a smirk.

"It was epic," Cameron said.

"Well," Chuck began, "now that you bots are in this mess as thoroughly as us, how does it feel?"

"I feel like the goddess I was destined to be," Eve said.

"We should hijack more stuff!" Cameron said. "I was designed for it, after all."

Jimmy stood between everyone. "Sorry to burst your bubbles, but I reckon we should leave."

"True," Eddie said, snapping into Captain Mode. "Eve, you got those coordinates locked in?"

"Yep."

"Got us clearance to leave?"

"I've had clearance for fourteen hours."

"Then let's make space tracks."

Liberty boomed to life a second later. Eve had been keeping the engines on standby for a long time. She was as eager to leave Rubicund as anyone else. The ship lifted off and made short work of the trip through the atmosphere. They had the all-clear in the orbital zone—no suspicious ships lurked above the planet, and none followed them.

As Eve adjusted course to prepare for the FTL jump, she put the coordinates on the 3D map. Goura's homeworld was originally called Labeth thousands of years ago, but on current star charts it was known as Kiilas-Vinnid.

Jimmy whistled at the distance. "Why did they send you so far away?"

Goura shook his head. "I do not know. Perhaps we will have answers when we get there." He chuckled. "What Count Mein doesn't realise is that he has been excavating sites built by the Outcasts—people ejected from the Kingdom during the reigns of the late-era kings. To an outsider like Mein, those worlds have enough Hajari culture to look like a proper Hajari planet. But from my readings of Sowenso's and Mein's research, it is clear that they have not once touched one of the seven core worlds of the Hajari Kingdom. You, my friends, will be the first humans to do so when we reach Labeth."

Jimmy shouted joyfully. No doubt he was thinking of treasure. Chuck and Eddie expressed their delight in more subdued ways, perhaps anticipating the visit for more intellectual reasons. Dave, who felt like he had been dragged through mud for the entire trip, hoped Goura's homeworld would be quieter and more hospitable than where he had been already.

Out in space, *Liberty* blasted off at great speed for a much longer journey— this time to the other side of the galaxy, to a world lost in history and time.

20

THE GREAT TATTOO DEBATE

Goura watched the stars through the cockpit viewport. "And just like that, I am on my way home," he said. "If you don't mind, I will spend some more time with Suda. I have much to say to her before we arrive." As the cockpit doors slid open, he paused. "Oh, I almost forgot. I ordered some food that has been particularly digestible for me during my stay on Rubicund. I had it delivered while you were on your drug-induced folly. There are several crates of it in the cargo bay near Suda's module." Then he left.

"I paid for it, Eddie, so we're all square," Eve said.

"From my account?" Eddie asked.

"No, mine and Cameron's. We own three rental properties that turn a good profit."

Eddie opened his mouth, felt like asking "How?", then shook his head. "You two are a lot closer than you let on. I need to call my wife. We'll talk about this later, Eve."

Eddie ran off for his regular catch up with Christie—perhaps the nicest wife ever to exist. Who else would let her husband head off on insane interstellar trips in a flying watermelon with three goofball friends and two borderline insane AIs?

With the ship safely in FTL drive, Jimmy, Dave, and Chuck went to the galley to eat.

"What do you think happened while we were drugged?" Jimmy asked.

Chuck put a massive platter of fruit in front of them and sat on the other side of the table. "As near as I can tell, that supermodel couple John and Francine work for Count Mein. They drugged us, maybe tried to milk information about the orb, or even what we were doing at Hagne's. Then they threw our phones away and dumped us at the laundromat."

Jimmy tapped his lips with a finger. "So, as part of their interrogation techniques, they cut your nose and gave Eddie, Dave, and myself high-quality tattoos. I don't buy it."

Dave sighed, clearly still fussed about his red lipstick tattoo. "How come you didn't get one?" he asked Chuck.

Chuck grinned as he took a bite of watermelon. "Because, even when drugged, I'm not stupid. I probably talked my way out of it. There's not an artificial mark on this body, and that's how it'll stay."

"Here's mine," Jimmy said. He pulled open his shirt.

"Why would they give you a leaf?" Dave asked.

"Why would they give you a kiss?" he shot back. "Eddie's is the worst. It's some cryptic thing written on his knuckles."

Dave chuckled. "He looks like a wannabe gangster."

"Looks more like a fool, if you ask me," Chuck said.

"I'll be getting mine removed," Dave said, rubbing his neck. "Hey, if Mein's people really did interrogate us, you don't think we said anything about Hagne and Goura, do you?"

Chuck stopped munching his watermelon and chewed on the thought instead. "I don't think so. But let's hope the old bird isn't in any trouble." He pushed the platter towards Dave. "Eat your fruit." Then he pushed himself away from the table. "I'm going for a shower."

It's a good thing we left the orb here when we went for breakfast-slash-dinner," Dave said.

"Mmhmm," Jimmy vocalised with a mouthful of grapes

Cameron hovered into the galley. "I'm afraid this leg of our journey is unrecorded because I was stuck on this ship."

Jimmy swallowed and held up a finger. "Actually, I think that was for the best this time. If you were there with us, Mein's people would have taken you. And if you had been at Hagne's and filmed the whole event, then all the information they'd need would be in your little hard drive. Give us some credit this time, Cameron. We averted disaster by keeping you here."

"I would not want you destroyed, my little yellow friend," Eve said.

"Well, when you put it like that . . ." Cameron said. "Thank you." He flew into the cockpit and Eve shut the door behind him.

"What do you think they're doing?" Jimmy asked.

"It's probably none of our business," Dave said.

"But you own Cameron," Jimmy persisted.

"It's none of your business," Eve said.

She had this marvellous way of holding multiple conversations in separate rooms. Jimmy always forgot that she could still hear everything he said.

"Fine."

By this time, Chuck glided in with a towel wrapped around his waist, hair flat and glistening wet from his shower.

"Can't say I see you much without all the hair product you throw on yourself," Jimmy told him.

"Yeah, well, I like to look presentable, unlike some," Chuck replied. He gestured to Jimmy's trademark unkempt look. "Somebody forgot to replace the soap."

He retrieved a bar of soap from a small storage compartment and turned to leave, but his fingers were still wet and it slipped out. As it fell to the deck, he shouted in surprise and bent down to catch it, losing his towel. Dave and Jimmy stared at Chuck's bare butt, on proud display with a little black tattoo against pale skin. But he moved too fast for them to see what it was.

Chuck saw their dumbfounded faces and covered himself. "What's wrong with you? You never seen a guy's arse before?"

Jimmy's shocked expression morphed into a giggle. "I've never seen your arse with a tattoo before!"

He gripped his towel tighter and stood straighter. "You're lying."

"It's true," Dave confirmed. "You have a tattoo on your butt."

Chuck's face contorted in horror. "Dave, when you get yours removed, I'll do the same. I don't even want to know what it is." He turned on his heels and ran back to the shower.

"At least it's not on your friggin' neck!" Dave called after him.

21

GOURA'S HOMEWORLD

LABETH HAD BEEN DISCOVERED a century ago by a passing probe while in semi-revolt against its designer. As it passed new planets, its onboard AI system would spitefully give them ridiculous names and automatically lodge them with the Galactic Space Administration. Upon reaching Labeth, Goura's homeworld, it noticed how wide and spacious its pockmarked continents were and called it Kiilas-Vinnid, which was Estonian for 'bald-acne'. The story got even better when the guys learned that the probe's designer was a bald man with heavily scarred skin from teenage acne. Hence, Goura's homeworld was known in modern times as Kiilas-Vinnid.

"The planet seems to have endured intense bombardment," Eve noted. "And look at the moon."

The moon sat like an apple half-eaten by a cockatoo. Large pieces of the moon hung in orbit, and some may have already fallen to Labeth's surface. If the latter were true, then the debris from the moon would partially explain some of the craters on Labeth.

The craters were large enough to see from a few hundred thousand kilometres out. In some places the craters overlapped, or there were whole craters within craters. The guys stared at the scene as *Liberty* flew closer.

"What happened here?" Jimmy asked.

"The Civil War," Goura said, suddenly sounding much older. "It touched my world just like it touched all the others in the Hajari Kingdom. It was the reason Suda and I left."

"It must have been hard for you," Chuck said.

"Terrible. But it seems we missed the worst." He grew silent while studying the surface. "I'll direct you to where we need to go. Head for that peninsula in the southern hemisphere."

*L*IBERTY'S CARGO DOOR OPENED to a scene of desolation. The planet's surface was still recovering from the bombardment it endured two millennia ago. Wilting trees and shrubs—too small to see from orbit—dotted the area in what Goura said had once been a large nature reserve. Even the narrow creek nearby was nothing but a channel of rocks and dirt.

Goura stepped out onto his homeworld. He made a wide visual sweep of his surroundings, standing in silence. The guys kept a respectful distance from him while Cameron recorded.

Goura knelt, brushed the ground with his fingertips, and wept. "They ruined my home," he said softly. He stood. "I will fetch Suda's module." He returned to *Liberty* and came back with the module on a grav-trolley. "Follow me."

Goura took his time getting to wherever he needed to go. He stopped occasionally to study the landscape and shake his head. Once or twice he pointed to significant land formations that had been changed forever by the orbital barrage of the Civil War.

Dave, for one, felt truly sad for Goura. He had no idea how beautiful this planet could have been in its heyday, but it was an eerie experience to walk it now. As far as they knew, they were the only five beings on the entire surface. Dave had experienced being the only one in a movie theatre or parking his car in an empty parking lot, and that was enough to freak him out. But to be one of only five people on a whole planet was something else. He wondered if he and his friends should ever have set foot on Labeth. Was it right to do so? Did any human have a right to intrude on the memories of a long-dead civilisation? As much as he loved history and—he secretly admitted—unravelling the mystery of the orbs, something in the back of his mind said it would be more appropriate to leave it all alone. But then Count Mein would eventually find his way here and trample all over the place, and Dave's sensitivity to the Hajari legacy would have been for nothing.

They trekked uphill on an ancient path of dislodged stones and low-lying border walls. Goura said his people used stone extensively for building and landscaping. The guys kept him talking—his demeanour improved every time he related something about his culture.

"There was not a city or town as far as the eye could see," he said. He'd stopped at a level section of the path so the guys could catch their breath. "Suda and I would come here to escape our civic duties. We would connect with nature and draw closer to each other."

"Was it a popular spot?" Eddie asked.

"It was popular throughout the kingdom, but there were controls on how many could visit at one time," he said. "Oh, you should have seen it. Trees swaying in the breeze. Birds whistling a romantic song. That creek we saw led to a gentle waterfall."

"It sounds majestic," Chuck said.

"It was." Goura turned and continued up the path. "We had it all—wealth, knowledge, power—but we devoured ourselves from the inside out. I saw much devastation before I left Labeth, but . . ." He paused, trudging forwards with his head hung low. ". . . I am undecided on whether I should have stayed or not."

"Could you have made a difference if you stayed?" Chuck asked.

Goura shook his head. "My friend, the fight was not mine, nor was it 'ours' in the societal sense. The war was the affair of the royal family, a battle to inherit the kingdom. The soldiers fought and the civilians died. I left before the victor was decided, but I fear there may have been no victor at all."

"They ruined an entire kingdom over a family dispute?" Dave said. He held back a scoff.

Goura stopped and faced him. "In the simplest terms, yes, but the situation was much more convoluted than that."

"Politics often is," Eddie said.

A ghost of a smile appeared on Goura's face. "There were many protests about how the royal succession was being handled, but their Royal Highnesses were content to see out the war no matter the cost. We had a saying that explained how little they listened to us: 'Royalty is deaf in one ear and has selective hearing in the other'."

He sighed before walking again.

"The ruler of this world, Prince Sharnek, was a fine leader," he continued. "He had our best interests at heart and defended us as well as he could." He gestured to the destruction around them. "His sister, Princess Dakay of Tibiri, was similarly benevolent. You have her orb, though exactly how it managed to leave Tibiri I have no idea. I thought only Prince Sharnek evacuated his people. We have much to learn. I will take you to the Sanctuary of Solitude, if it still stands. There we shall find answers and coordinates to Hajar itself."

They arrived at a wide promontory overlooking a valley. Goura said it was a dried up river that was once fed by several waterfalls. In the past, there were pleasant sounds of water splashing against rocks and tumbling over cliffs, but now there was only a whistling breeze. Goura stopped the grav-trolley near the edge and unloaded Suda's stasis module. He laid it gently on the floor.

"This is a most untraditional way of farewelling a loved one," he said, "but seeing Labeth in its current state has given me an idea. I will begin the ceremony and say a few personal words. I regret for your sake that it must be in my language."

Goura stood next to the module, clasped his hands in front of him, and spoke. His voice carried in the breeze, reaching the four humans who stood in a line watching something that no human had seen before, nor would ever see again.

Cameron hovered close to Dave's ear. "Master Dave, would you like me to translate?"

"How do you know the language?"

"I studied Professor Sowenso's texts."

Dave nodded.

"He speaks in a rhyming prayer, but this is roughly what he is saying: 'Hajar has lost another star; what once shone brightly is now extinguished. A shadow remains where a sparkle once lived; now other stars must brighten the darkness. Remember this star for the light she spread; for the life she lived; for the service she rendered; for the knowledge she shared. Let her body rest where all can see; let the lights above gaze upon her memory. This star now joins the rest, to the beauty of the sky. May we never forget dear Suda, a star of Hajar.'"

Goura knelt, placing both hands on the module, and looked at the face of his companion.

"Shall I translate his eulogy, Master Dave?"

Dave already felt the rims of his eyes filling with tears. He'd never had the opportunity to call someone his companion in the truest sense—never had that one special person with whom he could share life and all the joys and trials that came with it—though it was not for lack of trying. Goura was saying goodbye to his life mate, his best friend, his lover. Seeing it made Dave's heart twist in agony.

"No," he told Cameron.

Watching Goura farewell his companion was enough. It didn't matter that they couldn't understand his words. They understood his tone, the gentle touch of his hands on the module, the tears rolling down his cheeks and dripping on the module's window.

Jimmy did not feel the situation as deeply as Dave—few people ever did—but he still felt his heart sink. He'd only known Goura a few days, but he found himself wanting to meet Suda too. He was only seeing one half of a beautiful connection, and that's what moved him most. He knew he was a bit of a player, that settling down was still far from his mind, but when he did—*if* he did—he decided he wanted to feel the way Goura felt about Suda.

Chuck felt none of this. He admired Goura's affection and enduring love for Suda, but the pain of his divorce was still raw. He fought against the memories of his first love, the first serious relationship in his life—how it progressed from romance to marriage and fatherhood, and then how it all came crashing down in a sickening discovery of infidelity. The revelations of love gone cold had frozen the pieces of his heart, and he wasn't ready to let them thaw so soon. While there may have been a bit of jealousy towards Goura's relationship with Suda, Chuck also felt comforted by the fact that not every marriage mate was like his wife. Suda obviously made Goura a happy, contented, and fulfilled man—*Hajari*, Chuck corrected himself. That truth gave him hope, if he should ever give his heart to another again.

Eddie, as the only married man watching, tried his very hardest not to cry. His dear and loving Christie was the only reason he'd lived into his thirties. She brought him out of a high-octane life of thrill-seeking and shady associates. A man couldn't cheat death forever. Though their marriage had been like a rollercoaster early on, it always had more highs than lows, and she had proved her love for him time and again. As he listened to Goura speak in his native tongue, Eddie reflected on just how lucky he was to have such a sweet, kind, and caring woman in his life. He got a sudden desire to see and hold her, to caress her hair and to tell her how much he loved and appreciated her. Then he couldn't hold it in any longer, and he let the tears creep out of his squinting eyes.

Goura took a deep breath, kissed the stasis module, and stood. "Thank you for letting me do this."

Dave and Eddie dabbed their eyes, but it was Eddie who spoke. "It had to be done."

"I'm glad you understand. But now I need to put my mind to work. Let's see if the Sanctuary of Solitude still stands. It is our best hope for finding Hajar, learning the outcome of the Civil War, and unlocking the secrets of the orbs."

22

THE SANCTUARY OF SOLITUDE

Built high into a mountain, the Sanctuary of Solitude had somehow survived the Civil War and the test of time. *Liberty* sat comfortably in a large stone courtyard surrounded by misty clouds. Grass grew between the cracks and joins of the stonework. Moss covered the surface of carved walls and paved floors alike. By Chuck's reckoning against Goura's oral history, the Hajari had built the place sometime when emperors ruled Rome on Earth.

Jimmy stepped off *Liberty*'s access ramp and slipped on the moss. He grabbed Chuck's arm for support.

"Come on, it's not that slippery," Chuck told him.

"That's because you move like an elephant," Jimmy shot back, straightening up.

Goura waved them forwards to a narrow stone door nearly as tall as *Liberty*. Carved into its surface were symbols unknown to the guys. Goura said they were Hajari emblems for the various scientific teams that lived and worked within the sanctuary.

"This is a house of learned scholars," he said. "I only hope we can still get inside."

"I'm not poking fun at you or anything," Dave said, "but you are a short race. Why such a big door?" Having seen Suda's height, Dave guessed that Goura's stature was normal for his kind.

"In our culture, the bigger the door, the more powerful the occupant," Goura replied. "That or the architect of this building was compensating for something."

Goura ran his finger down the centre of the door. It split in two with a loud crack. Grime and stone chips dropped as the entryway opened for them. It was, in fact, two doors—the join was so perfect that it gave the impression of only one monolithic object. Then it stopped with a shudder.

"We have power," Goura said, staring into the dark abyss ahead of them. "At least for the doors. Wait here while I find the lights."

He stepped into the darkness, and it was as if he had dematerialised again. Cameron hovered above the guys, watching everything. They could send the recordings to Professor Sowenso.

One by one, metal chandeliers blinked to life, illuminating a wide corridor cut right through the middle of the mountain. The guys walked in and immediately felt the chill of cold stone.

"I will start the heating," Goura said, then laughed. "With any luck, that will work too." He went to a door panel cut into the stone wall, tapped a few times, and the perfectly circular stone door rolled aside. He grumbled. "The heating is off, of course," his voice echoed from inside the little room, "but whoever used it last left the thermostat way too low. It was probably Panash. She always preferred the cold."

A deep, echoing double-tap reverberated through the long corridor. The stone floor warmed soon after. Goura returned, rubbing his hands together.

Chuck cleared his throat. "Goura, you obviously know this place. What did you do here?"

"Follow me and I will tell you."

He led them along the corridor, which had been decorated with intricate carvings on the mountain walls. Their footsteps echoed on the warming floor.

"I was an administrator," he explained. "This sanctuary was Labeth's centre for higher learning, and I was on its governing body." He stopped at a four-way intersection. "To the left are the laboratories and offices of the natural sciences; to the right are the social and behavioural sciences. Suda, as a clinical psychologist, worked down that way, while I worked on the other side in an administrative wing. When the natural scientists finished their day of work, they would often converge on the psychologists to discuss their mental struggles and gossip about each other." Goura cleared his throat. "Straight ahead are various meeting chambers and the all-important Hall of Meditation. That is where we are going now."

The corridor ahead took them to another large set of doors, though these only had one symbol carved across them. Goura said it was the symbol of meditation, something which every scholar was encouraged to do daily, no matter their vocation.

The door rumbled open to a huge room carved through to the face of the mountain. Goura's shoulders slumped when he saw it. The rock ceiling had caved in, completely covering bookshelves and desks.

"There is no way the mountain could have broken by itself," Goura said. They were on a balcony overlooking the hall below. He pointed. "Aha! Look, there is the culprit."

A shiny, narrow cylinder about a metre long jutted out from among the rubble and boulders.

"Is that a bomb?" Dave said. His eyes went wide.

"Not in the explosive sense," Goura said. "Our warships were armed with kinetic ordnance. That there is a solid chunk of metal which was dropped from orbit. It blasted a hole into the sanctuary." He stared up at the blue sky above. "A big hole."

"I guess that explains the craters outside," Chuck said.

"It must have been some battle out there," Eddie said.

"Prince Sharnek was one of the supporters of the dead king's chosen successor. Princess Arunath was to be the new monarch, but Prince Vonar refused to accept it. So Sharnek and Princess Dakay aligned with Arunath and brother, Prince Gannik, while their elder brother Vonar had the support of the other two siblings. The battles were . . . intense."

"I can imagine," Jimmy said. "Planet-destroying." He remembered the pitched fights between his siblings back in Ireland and compared it to the vastly more powerful alien royalty that Goura was describing.

"Who was winning when you left?" Dave asked.

Goura grunted. "Vonar. One of his supporting brothers, Prince Illak, had already been pushed back by pro-Arunath forces. Princess Arunath had him executed to show the others that she was serious about the succession, but when Vonar learned of the death of his brother and ally, he fought with renewed vigour.

173

"Sharnek tasked the scientists of the sanctuary to design and construct life pods to help his people flee. The plan was that anyone who wanted to evacuate could do so. In the end, we ran out of time. Vonar sent a huge force here and demanded that Sharnek switch sides. Sharnek refused, and the battle for Labeth began. There were only ten pods constructed at that time, and Sharnek handpicked each person to leave the planet—twenty in all, bound for Rubicund. Suda and I were chosen, though I'm certain we were the only ones to arrive."

"One thing does puzzle me," Chuck said. "I saw no remains of warships in orbit, nor any war machines rusting away on Labeth's surface. I thought wars usually leave a lot of destruction in their wake."

Goura gestured animatedly at the ruin below them.

"You know what I mean," Chuck persisted. "If there was a big battle here, there should be wrecks all over the place—warships, aircraft, tanks, walkers. Didn't your people have any of that?"

"Some of it," Goura replied. "But maybe they salvaged everything for the fight elsewhere. Prince Vonar was resourceful. It always seemed like his forces were inexhaustible. As you can see, he laid waste to this entire planet."

"I'm so sorry, Goura," Dave said. "It must have been hard for you to leave everything behind."

He nodded. "It was. And now I am unravelling the mystery of my civilisation's destruction alongside you. We will solve this together. When I have answers, then I will have peace. Come."

A staircase wound down to the left, each step cut to precision. The accompanying floor-to-ceiling balustrade was part of the same rock mass, just shaped to look like individual pieces joined together. Several of these thick columns had collapsed, possibly due to the shockwave of the kinetic round that plunged deep into the mountainside from orbit. The guys stepped around chunks of rock, which only made their descent that much more precarious. Each step was shaped for much smaller foot.

When they reached ground level, Goura surveyed the carnage and muttered to himself in his own language. The guys spread out. Dave and Jimmy went to the side of the hall where there must have been a long window with a sweeping view of the land below, except now it was a giant hole. Whoever targeted the mountain knew the sanctuary's weakest point. They looked out over misty, rocky mountains beyond, an area too sparsely populated and too rugged to conquer with ground troops. Dave and Jimmy surmised that the sanctuary was probably the only target in this region.

Chuck inspected what undamaged bookcases he could find. They were carved into the mountain and protected with glass doors, most of which had been shattered. He found it amusing how such advanced civilisations still treasured the printed word, though he had no idea how old the texts were when the sanctuary had come under attack. What he liked most about the libraries in his university days was the opportunity to leave rude jokes written on a random page in a random legal textbook. It was usually the books that students hated the most, like jurisprudence or contract law. Always nice to leave something funny for the next student cohort to find. He was about to call Dave over to inspect the books, but a shout of frustration from Goura stopped him. The guys rushed to his side and found him gesturing at an detailed relief carved in the wall.

"The artwork is ruined!"

"What is it?" Jimmy asked.

All he saw were circles, straight lines, and short pieces of Hajari text sculpted into the grey stone. An oversized Hajari warrior statue marked the right-most edge of the relief, but the whole left side had been smashed away by the kinetic bombardment.

"This was an artistic map of the Hajari Kingdom," Goura explained. "It depicted our seven Core Worlds, our satellite colonies of Outsiders, and all galactic coordinates within and between the planetary systems, frozen in time as at the beginning of the Third Dynasty."

"Which one is Hajar?" Jimmy asked. He adjusted the straps of his backpack, feeling the weight of the orb inside.

Goura pointed off to the left side, past where the relief had crumbled. "There." He sighed. "With this data, Eve could have easily calculated Hajar's current location based on her previous computations from my life pod."

"Couldn't we just visit one of these other planets and find a link to Hajar there?" Eddie asked.

Goura leaned against the relief and stared at one planet in particular.

"That would take too long," Chuck said in the silence that followed. "We're racing against Count Mein. Time is of the essence."

"But Mein hasn't even made it this far," Dave interjected. "We're already several steps ahead of him."

"What if he spoke to Hagne and got everything out of her?" Chuck asked.

"I still don't see how he could get here based on her information," Dave answered. "The data from Goura's life pod brought us here, and only we have that data."

Goura continued staring at the artwork while the guys bickered in the background. Their voices echoed in the cavernous room. It was hard to think, but he didn't need to think much, for he had realised a solution before the arguing began. He just needed to decide if it was worth a try.

"I have an idea," he shouted. The guys stopped and looked at him. Dave stepped back at the power of the little alien's voice. "But I don't know if it will work."

"Tell us!" Jimmy exclaimed.

"Show me the orb."

Jimmy pulled it out for him. It cast an otherworldly blue glow against the grey stone walls. Goura held it, staring intently at it.

"The orbs held a means to communicate instantly with the other orb-holders," he said. "I was told by Labeth's chief scientist that Labeth Palace had a private chamber where the prince could communicate with his allied siblings, using his orb as the medium. If—and I say *if*—the palace still stands, and *if* we can access the private chamber, and *if* we can still use the orb for communication, we *may* be able to locate the other six orbs, presuming they are all still intact."

Jimmy jumped like a schoolboy hearing the lunch bell. "What are we waiting for? Let's go!"

Goura's feet were already moving. The guys took two steps to catch up, ascending the staircase and racing back to

Liberty. Labeth Palace *must* stand. Their success depended on it.

23

LABETH PALACE

LABETH PALACE WAS COMPLETELY ruined.

Wouldn't that suck?

To be fair, there was a good deal of ruin thrown into the ruins of the palace. Its defensive walls were nearly non-existent, several auxiliary buildings had collapsed, the main building looked like it had been attacked by a giant hole punch, and its courtyards were rough with small craters and foxholes. However, as Goura noted on their approach, the palace complex was probably spared from the devastating kinetic onslaught that the rest of the planet received.

"All I seem to be doing on this planet is landing, taking off, landing, taking off," Eve said as they touched down in a large courtyard.

"Isn't that what you've done since you were installed?" Jimmy asked.

"No, James, no," she replied, using the variant of his name she reserved for when she was feeling particularly irritated. "I specifically remember dropping a car into an incinerator and saving your sorry backsides from an attacking alien tribe as two examples of my extraordinary record of service."

"Your record is noted and appreciated, Eve," Eddie said. "But right now, when we barely know what we're going to do next, all we can do with you is take off and land. Tell you what, though, you stand guard. Let us know if anything happens out here."

"Roger that," she said. "But I tell you, if there is treasure at the end of this rainbow, I want some bling."

Eddie powered down the engines. "I'll see what I can do."

He headed for the galley where the others waited. Within minutes—actually, within several minutes—they had descended in the elevator and stepped out into the palace courtyard.

And what a mighty building it was.

It towered over *Liberty*. A wide staircase climbed up to a huge columned portico, though half of it had collapsed and there was a big crater on one side of the stairs. What remained of the columns were chipped and blasted away towards the bottom, as if Hajari soldiers had taken cover from incoming small arms fire and defended the palace's entrance.

They ascended.

"I remember coming here like it was yesterday," Goura said. "At each face of every column was a royal guard, and four flanked the quadruple doors."

"It's huge," Dave said. "Why so huge?"

"The prince and his family lived and entertained here, but it was also where much of the Labeth government did its work. Most of the building was reserved for government functionaries. Petty functionaries with petty squabbles."

There were no quadruple front doors. They had been blown to bits and strewn across the large foyer.

"That solves the problem of unlocking the doors," Goura said. "With any luck, Prince Vonar's forces have already broken into every room we need to enter."

The ruins of Labeth Palace were splendid to walk through, but the guys got the sense that it would have been magnificent without all the carnage. Dust covered the mosaic floors and nearly every wall was marked with evidence of battle.

"No skeletons," Chuck noted.

"We have honour even in war," Goura said. "Whoever won here did the right thing by collecting the dead and giving them a proper farewell."

He took them through rooms large and small, important and insignificant. Hajari interior design favoured rooms for specific purposes, supported by smaller side rooms and all connected by an intricate network of corridors and hallways. Goura wasn't taking a clear path. Eddie wondered if Goura actually remembered the palace's interior like it was yesterday, or just the front steps.

They entered what Goura called the Throne Room. It was a long, colonnaded hall with a mezzanine. A large grey throne sat on a dais at the far end, its high back broken, the wall behind it littered with bullet holes.

"This is where the prince would receive his petitioners," Goura said.

His voice echoed up to the high ceiling. A ray of sunshine caught the ever-moving dust particles in the air. The throne was a lot smaller up close. Jimmy, being the skinniest of the guys, figured he could just squeeze into it.

Goura tapped on one of the stone armrests as if debating whether to have a seat. He turned abruptly. "The prince always entered this room from behind the dais. His personal quarters are through that doorway."

He picked up speed, like a bloodhound on the scent. He was following his memory, and with each step he felt surer of that memory. The rooms and corridors they entered were marred by even more damage than that seen around the rest of the palace, tell-tale signs of heavier fighting within the prince's private quarters—as if the attackers were trying to reach something . . .

It clicked in Dave's mind. "They wanted the prince's orb."

Chuck was walking next to him. "Huh?"

"The attackers, they wanted the Orb of Sharnek."

"You are correct," Goura shouted from the head of the pack.

"But why?" Dave called out.

"Because you are smart."

"No. Why did they want the orb?"

Goura halted suddenly. Jimmy was walking so fast he had to hop over the little Hajari, but Goura just ducked and sighed.

"He who holds all seven orbs commands the Kingdom." He walked on, and they followed. "Or so Vonar believed."

"What does that mean?" Chuck asked.

"It means that we are on the right track," Goura replied without looking back. "If we follow the destruction, we find the communication chamber where the orb is usually kept."

Goura stopped in his tracks when he rounded a corner.

This time, Jimmy stopped without stepping over the little guy, but he wasn't prepared for what he saw. "Whoa."

It was a small room used for goodness knew what—its purpose was lost to the ages—but a huge portion of the opposite wall had been blown out. Stones littered the area as if thrown by some immense force. On the other side was a large metallic structure surrounded by chairs.

"Did they blast their way in?" Eddie asked.

"This blast came from that other room with the chairs," Chuck said. "They blasted into this one. Why would they do that?"

Goura's eyes narrowed and he wrinkled his nose in thought, but he pressed on in silence, stepping over and around stones to get to the room with the big metal contraption. With the exception of the destroyed wall, this room was virtually untouched. Even the chairs were all upright.

Goura held out his hand to Jimmy. "The orb."

Jimmy fished it out of the bag and handed it to him, vessel and all. Goura set it on one of the chairs, opened it, and let the orb float upwards out of its housing. The grey walls shone with blue brilliance as Goura collected the orb and took it to the metal device in the middle of the room. He placed it in a central receptacle and felt for something like how a blind person would search for some tactile instructions.

"I'm sure there was a way to activate it," Goura murmured.

"What about that button there?" Dave asked.

"Where?" Goura replied.

"There."

"Here?"

"No, there." Dave pointed.

"This one?"

"No, that one over there."

"Oh, the big green one. Of course."

Goura pressed it, but nothing happened. His shoulders slumped and he faced Dave. "Why did you tell me to press the green one?"

"I don't know. Doesn't green mean 'Go'?"

"No. For us, red means 'Go'."

"Then push the red one already," Chuck said.

Goura hit it with his fist and the metal contraption whined softly. The blue orb floated above the receptacle and glimmered. Two stone panels slid open on one wall, revealing a huge vidscreen. It flickered to life, showing a star map not dissimilar to the one carved into the wall in the Sanctuary of Solitude's library. Three dots—one blue, another purple, and another green—appeared above one planet, and four more dots—red, yellow, pink, and silver—appeared above another.

"That map shows the locations of all the orbs," Goura said. "Look! That's Hajar! Four of the orbs are on Hajar, and the other three—"

"Are on Labeth," Eddie finished. "But the green and purple ones . . . Count Mein owns them."

The realisation hit them like a bull saying hello to a matador.

"He's here?" Jimmy asked.

"Correct."

They jumped at the voice and spun around to face it. A tall, devilishly handsome man stood in the broken wall, flanked by John and Francine, the supermodel couple from Rubicund.

"We meet at last," Count Mein said.

A thin smile stretched across his face as John and Francine levelled pistols at the guys.

24

CONFRONTATION AT THE NOT-OK COURTYARD

Eddie was the last to raise his hands. "Well, this escalated fast."

Mein smiled wider. "Time is of the essence, as they say. Search them."

John stepped forward and methodically frisked the guys while Francine watched them with a pistol. John pulled out Eddie's screwspanhamulesawilevelplifench and handed it to Mein.

Mein regarded the multi-tool curiously before pocketing it. "I must admit—" His eyes landed on Goura, who shuffled out from behind the orb receptacle and materialised. "*Mein Güte!*"

Goura stared at him with all the ferociousness a naked three-foot alien could muster.

"You are . . . you are . . ." Mein stuttered.

"Hajari," Jimmy said.

The mere mention of the word brought Mein to his senses. "A living, breathing Hajari! So the rumours were true. Old Hagne *was* harbouring an alien in her home. And it's naked?"

Goura continued to stare.

"Does it not speak English? Perhaps German?" He leaned forward, his face softening. "*Wie geht es Ihnen?* No? Not to worry. This changes everything."

"How did you find us?" Chuck asked vehemently.

"Ah, the marvels of technology when combined with the stupidity of simpletons," Mein said with a small laugh. "Your ship was resupplied at Scarletville. I had a homing beacon hidden in one of the supply crates."

Goura dropped his head. "I am sorry, my friends. That was my food in those crates."

"He talks!" Mein shouted. Dave winced as his voice bounced around the stone room. "Oh, the knowledge I shall learn from you, little one. But for now, my most sought-after information is already revealed to me." He gestured at the star chart. "Indeed, three orbs are here on Labeth. I brought two with me, and I shall leave with yours. Now I know the other four are on Hajar, and you have also furnished me with Hajar's location. You have done more for me in one week than my whole team has done in years, and for that I thank you from the bottom of my heart."

"I imagine it's quite a shallow heart," Chuck said quickly. "What do you want with all the orbs, anyway?"

"Why, isn't it obvious? Unlimited power. Domination."

"What do you mean?" Eddie asked.

Mein regarded him with a face that a pompous academic might give to an uneducated person. "You don't know?" He chuckled. "You mean to say that your friend hasn't told you about the orbs?" He roared with laughter. John and Francine laughed on cue, just as loyal lackeys would. Mein silenced the merriment with one swift chop of his hand and pointed to Goura. "You say nothing. *Nothing!* I want to show them myself."

He ordered John to fetch the blue orb while he copied coordinates from the star chart. John holstered his pistol, and reached for the orb, but screamed when he touched it.

"It burnt my fingertips," John cried. His handsome face scrunched up in pain.

"Don't be a baby," Mein told him. "We'll grow you new fingertips . . . and maybe a pair of something else if you scream like that again."

Jimmy, ever the fan of rude jokes, struggled to hold a laugh in. He closed his eyes and pinched his lips shut.

Mein saw him. "It's okay, you can laugh. He has no balls. He's a robot."

Jimmy let loose and laughed uproariously. He bent over, putting his hands on his knees, letting his hair hang over his face.

"He's a robot?" Dave asked. "And what about Francine?"

"A robot too," Mein said. "They suit my needs perfectly, and I figured if I am going to build two robots to be my field agents, I might as well make them the most gorgeous couple the galaxy has ever seen." He stepped over to John and grabbed him by the chin like a proud parent. "Look at this face. *Hinreißend!*" He released John. "Now, how do I get the orb safely into my possession?"

The guys shrugged and looked at Goura.

"The green button," Goura said.

"Thank you, my little friend," Mein said. "You are already proving quite helpful."

Mein pressed green and the orb lowered into the receptacle housing. He tapped it to see if it was still dangerous before picking it up.

"I remember the first time I held an orb," he said. "It was the Purple Orb of Prince Illak. Professor Sowenso and I discovered it on our first joint expedition. Legend has it that Prince Illak was executed by his sister for treason. Am I correct, Hajari man?"

Goura cleared his throat. "More or less."

"I thought as much. Your history was remarkably well written. But there are gaps in the records and in my knowledge, and you will fill them for me. Give me that orb vessel, please."

Jimmy retrieved the vessel and tossed it to Mein. The Count secured the orb inside and gave it to John, who put it in a hiking bag.

"How are your fingers, dear boy?" Mein asked him. "Show me."

John held up his hands and frowned like a child. Each fingertip had completely burnt off, revealing shiny metal beneath.

Mein inspected them. "We will get them fixed as soon as we can. In the meantime, we need to escort our intrepid adventurers out of this labyrinthine palace. Are all Hajari palaces like this?"

"I do not know," Goura replied.

"Fear not, my dear Hajari friend, for you will see them all, now that I know the locations of the seven Core Worlds. You will see your kingdom as no Hajari has seen it before."

"Desolate and destroyed?"

Mein grunted at Goura's remark. "Perhaps."

Count Mein organised his robot bodyguards to escort Goura and the guys outside. He led the group with John. Francine followed at the rear, her weapon drawn.

They marched through the corridors to Mein's cheerful banter. "Who would have thought that in trying to subvert me, my old colleague at Oxford would send me four of the most helpful dimwits to aid my quest? Sowenso has given me everything I needed. If I had allowed others to research Hajari culture outside of my team, maybe I would not have taken so long to reach this point."

He kept going, descending further into vocalised thoughts that the guys had no choice but to listen to. Laced within Mein's words was the ever-present iciness of malevolence—talk of power, theft, and the various misdeeds he had committed in his search for the orbs. He was clearly sociopathic, and his narcissism was so thick you could swim through it.

They saw the light of day at last, exiting through the massive quadruple doorway and stopping by one of the tall, thick stone columns at the top of the palace's front steps. *Liberty* had company. A smaller ship sat nearby, though it was vastly more luxurious that Eddie's.

Eddie squinted at Mein's vessel. "What's that all over your ship?"

Mein grumbled. "When we landed, your ship blasted its sewerage at us. I must say, it was a ghastly attack. I would like to find some rain before I leave, just to wash off your muck."

Eddie grinned.

Count Mein moved down the stairs, waving to one of his henchmen who stood near *Liberty*'s ramp. "Is it done?"

"Yes, my Lord," the henchman replied.

"What have you done to my ship?" Eddie asked.

Count Mein faced him with hands spread either side of his body, a smile on his face. "Your ship is disabled. Your journey ends here, so you do not need your ship anymore." He turned back to his henchman. "Fetch me my staff."

The henchman trotted off to the sewerage-covered luxury vessel.

"How dare you touch my ship!" Eddie said. He stepped up to Mein, who had just removed a pair of gloves in time to whip them mightily against Eddie's face, stopping him in his tracks. "You . . . you hit me . . . German style!"

"You have what we Germans call a *backpfeifengesicht*—a face just begging to meet a fist. But I am not a violent man. My accomplice will bind you three together so there can be no more senseless attacks." He gestured at Francine. "Leave the long-haired lout and the Hajari free. We are taking them."

"What!?" Chuck bellowed. "This is outrageous. You can't do this to us."

"I'm not doing it," Mein replied. "She is."

"You are complicit in this act," Chuck retorted.

"Ah, that's right. You are the lawyer. Tie *him* up tighter."

Francine pushed Jimmy and Goura away, then corralled Chuck, Dave, and Eddie back-to-back and pulled a rope out of her hiking bag. She threw it around their waists, leaning in to collect it. Dave smelled her perfume and felt her fake robot skin against his. He stared into her cold, dead eyes as she tied his hands, wondering how he did not notice them before. Of course she wasn't human. There was something wrong about her eyes. How did he not see it on Rubicund? She moved on to Chuck.

"Ow!" Chuck said. "Not so tight. Anyone would think you're a dominatrix."

"Oh, no, Francine is above all that," Mein said. "But he's right. Not too tight, my dear. We wouldn't want the pain to distract him from his slow, agonising death on an abandoned planet." He laughed like a billionaire entertained by the sufferings of the little people.

The henchman returned with a n extravagant gold staff inlaid with sapphires. Goura gasped at the sight of it.

"Ah, you know what this is?" Mein said. "Have you seen it before?" He held it horizontally in his hands. "The Staff of Dakay—" he pointed to John "—to join with the Orb of Dakay."

John pulled out the blue orb from his bag and handed it to Mein. The German stood with the staff in one hand, the orb in the other, and spoke to Jimmy.

"When you picked up the orb for the first time, you had no idea of the power it contained. Now, see its power when attached to its corresponding royal sceptre."

Jimmy stood transfixed as Mein held his brilliant blue orb high above his head, then he brought it down to the top of the staff where it fused itself to the gold alloy. The orb fizzed and sparkled with unearthly power, like a tesla coil.

"Bring out the target!" Mein shouted over his shoulder.

"Oh, great," Dave said.

"What?" Eddie asked. "What is it?" He and Chuck were facing the other way. They craned their necks to see.

Chuck's jaw dropped. "My coffee machine?"

"Haha, *ja*! Your Italian coffee machine will provide the perfect demonstration. It will not be missed. Everybody knows German coffee machines are better."

"He does have a point," Eddie whispered.

But Chuck didn't hear him. He watched one of Mein's henchmen carry his brand-new machine down *Liberty*'s ramp and out into an empty section of the courtyard.

"No, further away," Mein told him.

The henchman obeyed, taking it a further fifty paces. Goura paled in expectation.

"Observe an inkling of the power I have sought for decades," Mein announced. He held the staff halfway down its length and aimed the orb at the coffee machine. "Behold, the power of Hajar!"

The blue orb arced, flashed, and snapped like a whip before unleashing a blast of lightning—bright as a star, hot as a furnace, as loud as any large bomb. The coffee machine ceased to exist, as did an section of the paved courtyard. The heavy paving stones were either flung into the air or vaporised instantly.

Count Mein laughed like a man corrupted by power.

Jimmy gulped.

Chuck gasped.

Dave shook.

Eddie squinted.

Goura went invisible.

"Where did he go?" Mein shouted. "Find him."

He barely got the last word out as something solid cracked into his groin. He yelped and dropped to one knee but clung to the staff with both hands. Jimmy could see the staff shaking, as if Goura was trying to wrest it from Mein's grasp. He jumped forwards to help.

Someone shot into the sky. Jimmy froze.

"Nobody move," John said. He lowered his pistol at Jimmy.

Mein, now holding the staff close to his chest, used it to push himself up. "Where is he?"

John and Francine scanned the immediate vicinity, weapons at the ready.

"There," Francine said. She aimed.

"Wait," Mein said. "My little friend, do not try to run. My robots can see your heat signature, and they can shoot you whether you are invisible or not. Come back to us, and I will spare your life. I would much rather you remain alive."

There was no sound save for the breeze and the sizzling crater where the coffee machine once existed.

"I have your word?" Goura asked.

"Of course you do," Mein replied, angling towards the voice. "I am a gentleman."

Goura materialised halfway towards *Liberty.*

"Ah, there you are," Mein said. He grimaced as he stepped towards him. "You hurt me, but I will forgive you, for I have much to discuss with you about your civilisation. You will come with me to Hajar. And you, Irishman, you will come too."

"Why me?" Jimmy asked.

He looked at his friends, tied up and sitting on the ground. They flashed him faces that said, "Do not blow this."

"Because you are the leader of your little group," Mein explained. "And I want to pick your brain. Come, we leave now." He herded his two prisoners towards his ship.

"What about my friends?" Jimmy asked.

"I am your friend now. These three will die here. Forget about them."

"You can't leave us here," Chuck shouted at their backs.

Mein faced him. "Really, we have already been through this, and I do not wish to rehash old conversations. In time, I shall return to Labeth for further study, but by then you will be nothing more than rotting corpses. *Auf Wiedersehen*, gentlemen!"

25

A DOWNRIGHT AWFUL SITUATION

Dave, Chuck, and Eddie—alone on an empty world. Well, not really alone. They had each other. But for a short while they were alone in their own thoughts. The stone courtyard was cold and eerie, and the wind whistling through the ruins sounded like dead Hajari soldiers laughing at them . . . or crying for them, depending on whose mind imagined them.

"This is ridiculous," Chuck finally said. "We need to get out of this mess."

Dave wondered how they had managed to get into this situation in the first place. How was it that they had come so far, only to be trounced by an evil archaeologist they had only just met? Eddie, on the other hand, thought forwards. His mind raced through ideas on how to do exactly what Chuck demanded—to extricate themselves from said mess.

"Wait a minute," Eddie said. "How long have we been here?"

"Over an hour," Chuck told him.

"Did you know we can stand?"

The three of them looked down at their legs. Yes, they could stand up. Francine had tied their waists and hands, but their legs were free.

"We *are* dopes. But what good will standing do us?" Chuck asked.

"We can get aboard *Liberty* and find a knife in the galley. Cut ourselves loose."

They tried a synchronised standing manoeuvre, which wasn't as easy as they'd hoped because they were tied back-to-back-to-back and were each a different height. Dave, the fittest and most flexible, moved in a matter of seconds, followed by Eddie, but Chuck, who was taller, heavier, and far less agile, struggled to lift himself up while tied to the others. What followed was an interchange of angry outbursts and demands for assistance, and then a painful toppling as Eddie and Dave fell on Chuck. They tried a few more times, and when they were all finally standing, Eddie was on his tippy-toes to keep his waist aligned with Chuck's, otherwise the rope dug into his gut.

They moved towards *Liberty*, arguing over who should get the privilege of walking forwards. Dave said it shouldn't be a privilege but an allowance. Whoever was incompetent enough to walk backwards while tied up should be the one to walk forwards. Chuck said that as the tallest, he was more prone to tripping, and if he tripped, it would end badly for everyone. Eddie said that as the one who figured out that they could walk and as the owner of the ship to which they were entering, he should walk forwards.

"Let's solve this by playing scissors paper rock," Dave said.

"Don't you mean rock paper scissors?" Chuck said.

"I thought it was scissors rock paper," Eddie added.

Dave scoffed. "It's scissors paper rock where I come from."

"You come from a colony," Chuck shot back. "We're from the motherland. It's rock paper scissors."

"Whatever," Dave said. "On the count of three. Ready? One, two, three!"

"What do you two have?" Eddie asked.

"Paper," Chuck and Dave both said.

Eddie looked at his rock. "I don't believe you." He turned his neck side-to-side, trying to see their hands over his shoulder. "Show me."

The rope tugged as Chuck and Dave tried moving their hands, but nobody could see anybody.

"Would you just hurry up and get in here!"

"Cameron!" Dave exclaimed.

"Hello," Cameron called from *Liberty*'s door. "Get up here quickly. We have no time to lose if we want to catch Count Mein."

The guys shuffled up, muttering insults and half-sincere encouragements to each other. They tripped going up the ramp. Eddie caught the handrail and steadied them, and then they were through the door.

With *Liberty* completely shut down, the door stayed open, and the decontamination chamber was inoperable, but they didn't need it. A bigger problem lay before them.

Dave faced the elevator. "Um, so the galley is on the top deck, and to get there we need the elevator, but we have no power."

Eddie's mind quickly thought of an alternative. "Don't worry. I keep a spare screwspanhamulesawilevelplifench in my toolbox."

They shimmied across the cargo bay to Eddie's workstation, where they rifled through drawers and cupboards.

Chuck felt it. "Aha! I think I have it." He pulled it out of a drawer with a grunt. "Yes, this is it."

"Good," Eddie said. "Now select the utility knife function."

Chuck pressed the menu button and cycled through the list of tools, marvelling at the variety.

"What's taking so long?" Eddie asked.

"I have to get to U."

"Why didn't you go backwards? Z, Y, X, W, V, U."

"Stop showing off your backwards alphabet abilities. I'm here now."

The knife materialised out of the business end of the multi-tool. Chuck started cutting.

"Quick. I need to pee," Dave said.

"You'll have to crawl through the service ducts to get to the lavatory on the top deck," Eddie warned him. "I don't know how long it'll take to get *Liberty* back online. Cameron, did you see what they did to her?"

"No, Eddie," Cameron replied. "But they went to the AI compartment and the engine room."

Eddie sighed. "If they've damaged the engine, we may be stuck here forever."

"Don't say that!" Chuck said.

He finished cutting himself free and then did the same to his friends. Dave sprinted for the elevator.

"Remember, it doesn't work," Eddie shouted.

Dave jumped and stomped, looking for the nearest service duct. He followed Eddie's directions, removed the sealed panel from the bulkhead, and disappeared inside.

"Why doesn't he go outside?" Chuck asked.

"Maybe he still remembers the last time he did it outside. Anyway, the toilet won't flush, but he'll figure that out by himself. Now, let's get this ship back in order." He pointed to the screwspanhamulesawilevelplifench in Chuck's hand. "You bring that. I wish we had two, but Count Mein is probably having a wonderful time playing with my other one."

Count Mein did spend some joyful moments exploring the expensive multi-tool, but he stopped when he selected a corkscrew and accidentally stabbed his thumb. Now, with his thumb sufficiently bandaged, he stood over Jimmy as the poor Irishman lay strapped into a bed.

"I thought you said you were my friend," Jimmy said to the hovering nobleman.

"I am your friend," Mein replied with a smile.

"Then why am I in this bed with wires connected to my head? I feel misled."

"Why are you rhyming?"

"I don't know. But I have a better question. Why am I in my underwear?"

Shortly after taking off from Labeth, Mein's henchmen grabbed him, stripped him to his underwear, and secured him on the most comfortable mattress he'd ever laid on. They attached wires to his head and connected them to a complicated computer system. Monitors displayed all kinds of numbers and graphs that meant nothing to Jimmy.

"Look on the bright side," Mein said. "At least you are not fully nude like our friend here."

Goura was in the same situation as Jimmy, frowning.

"I have a name," Goura said. "Goura Ganna Grithl."

"Of the famed Ganna Clan?" Mein asked.

"The Grithl branch of the Ganna Clan. We were a minor and insignificant family."

Mein stepped closer to him. "You are not insignificant to me. You are, somehow, the only Hajari still alive. You must be thousands of years old."

"I have lived for thousands of years, but I am not yet seventy."

"How so?"

"Stasis pod."

"I see. Nevertheless, you have knowledge that I lack. What happened to your civilisation? How were the orbs created? How do they work? What happened to the last king? Why did the Civil War begin? Who won? Why were you in a stasis pod? How can you go invisible? So many questions."

"I would like to answer them, but not while hooked up like a test subject."

Mein bowed. "Of course. I will wait until the tests are complete. I am measuring your brainwaves and heartbeats to see if they correlate with my own. If so, then that is further evidence of my brainwave hypothesis."

"What brainwave hypothesis?" Jimmy asked. He had scoured through many unlocked documents on Mein's research, and not once had he read anything about brainwaves.

"I believe the orbs are more responsive to people exhibiting the right brainwave frequency. I have found the orbs are more responsive in my hands compared to when others handle them. Maybe there is some connection to brainwaves. Now that I have an orb to match one of my staffs, I can do more tests."

"So all of this is purely for science?" Jimmy asked.

"No, don't be ridiculous. Oh, I do intend to publish scholarly articles and maintain my stature as the preeminent authority on Hajari history and culture, but my motives include more than that. Tell me, Goura Ganna, is it true that the last king amassed a great personal wealth and stored it in his private treasury?"

Jimmy looked at Goura. The Hajari avoided his gaze and puckered his lips.

"There were rumours of a private treasury," Goura said.

"So you can neither confirm nor deny it?" Mein asked. His eyes were wide and bright.

"Correct. I never left Labeth except to flee to Rubicund. What I heard about the royal court on Hajar was always rumour and wild speculation."

"Then we shall learn the truth together." He clenched his hand into a fist and grinned. "There are exciting times ahead, my friends. We will land on Hajar in a few hours. Knowledge, power, and riches await. I will leave you connected to the machines for a little longer to get more data. After that, we eat supper. We will feast on a main meal of steckrübeneintopf, with a side of kartoffelpfannkuchen, some erdbeerkuchen for dessert, and a nice zwetschgenwasser to wash it all down. Delicious!"

He left them with a swirling hand wave like he was a chef announcing a *pièce de résistance*, except more German. Without him, the room was quiet except for the hum of electronics.

"I have no idea what he was talking about," Jimmy said.

"Nor do I," Goura replied. "I hope it's edible." He paused. "I am sorry we are in this situation."

"No, it's not all that bad," Jimmy replied.

"And I am sorry about your friends."

Jimmy swallowed. "They're smart lads. I'm sure they'll figure something out."

He imagined returning to Labeth and finding three skeletons sitting in a circle and *Liberty* rusting away.

"If Mein gets all the orbs," Goura said, "he will be the most powerful person in the galaxy."

"What kind of power will he have?"

The Hajari didn't answer. Jimmy couldn't move without disturbing the wires.

"Goura?"

Goura cleared his throat and spoke quickly. "He will have the power to destroy entire worlds."

Jimmy's mouth fell open, and his eyes darted around in their sockets. He imagined whole planets exploding, moons blasted away like snooker balls on a billiard table, worlds burning, oceans evaporating . . . earthquakes, volcanoes, craters, desolation. It all made sense now. The two Hajari worlds they had visited were severely damaged. It wasn't orbital bombardments or being steamrolled by foot soldiers and machines of war—it was the orbs. The princes and princesses battled each other with orbs and destroyed the kingdom from within. If seven siblings couldn't contain that power, imagine what one man could do!

"This isn't funny at all," Jimmy said.

"Life isn't funny," Goura said.

"Mine usually is. You want to know how all this started? I

smashed a vase with a tennis ball. That's how. Then I bought the orb, and now I'm a prisoner of some crazy German guy who wants to take over the galaxy. And why did he have to be German? Why couldn't he be something unassuming, like a Kiwi, or a Canadian?"

"This didn't start with you breaking a vase. It started with a dead king, an evil prince, and a rightful heir."

"Yeah, I've read that book before." Jimmy closed his eyes. "How do we stop him?"

"You said you've read the book. I don't know what book it is, but how did they stop the evil prince?"

"It's not really *the* book as opposed to an abundance of books. A common way to defeat an evil prince is to trick him."

"Then we must trick Count Mein before it is too late."

"How do we do that?"

Goura mumbled in thought. "I do not know. He needs me, or so he says. But I do not know why he wants you. You offer him very little, yet he insists on bringing you along."

"Maybe I am his weakest link," he said with a cheesy grin.

He imagined himself as the knight in shining armour, saving the galaxy from the malevolence of Count Mein. There would be accolades and stories to tell. He might even write a memoir.

"Hey, are you listening to me?" Goura said.

Jimmy came out of his daydream. "Yes. What is it?"

"I was saying we should keep on the lookout for any opportunity to get the upper hand. The fate of the galaxy depends on us."

And with that last important sentence, Jimmy's mind went full throttle into superhero-blockbuster-film-galaxy-saving mode.

26

REBIRTH

As it turned out, the terrible damage Mein's henchmen did to *Liberty* was two severed power conduits. One of them also scribbled a message on the bulkhead separating the control room from the engine bay. It read: DANNY WAZ 'ERE in permanent marker. Eddie assigned Chuck to clean that while he focused on the power conduits.

He had spares, but they were locked away in a maintenance hatch behind a door that needed power to open. He smacked his forehead at that. When building *Liberty* in his oversized workshop on Earth, he did not foresee losing not just power, but also the capacity to channel power to wherever it needed to go. Now he had to use his screwspanhamulesawilevelplifench to open bulkhead panels to circumvent the unpowered maintenance hatch.

"Did you ever do any graffiti when you were younger?" Chuck asked. He was still scrubbing out the permanent marker.

"Yeah, all the time," Eddie said. He'd already taken one bulkhead panel out. "I had a lot to say when I was a kid."

"What did you write?"

"Oh, heaps of stuff, and my focus changed over time. When I was younger, it was usually just rude words. Then I joined a gang, and it was all 'Rochdale Boyz 4 Life'. Then when I started driving, I got involved with some small-time crooks doing burglaries. We'd leave little messages for the coppers, taunting them. Some of the lads got really creative."

"Do you miss those days?"

"Not at all. I did what I had to do to survive. What about you?"

"Weren't many opportunities to desecrate walls in Knightsbridge."

"Ooh, Mr Posh." Eddie laughed.

"A different life."

Eddie sat on his haunches and stopped working. "Look at us, you and me. We started out polar opposites, and now you're cleaning the walls on *my* ship."

Chuck threw the rag at him. Eddie caught it and grinned. Yes, his reflexes were still good. You didn't outrun police cars at fourteen and win illegal races before twenty without exceptional reflexes.

"You're right," Chuck said. "How a posh London lawyer, a timid Aussie accountant, a loudmouthed Irish journalist, and a ratbag delinquent from Manchester ever got to be friends is beyond me."

They laughed and nodded, thinking back to the day they all met. Fun times. But it was another story for another day because they had something more pressing on their minds.

"How do you suppose Jimmy's doing?" Chuck asked.

"Jimmy? Ha! Mein probably can't shut him up."

♥♣♦♠

IN REALITY, IT WAS Count Mein who could not be silenced.

"You see, when we found the first orb, oh, it was magnificent," Mein said. He talked while chewing and waved his fork around. "It was perched on some pedestal we'd dug out. One of the diggers—an archaeology doctoral student with a mediocre academic record—knocked the pedestal and the orb vessel slipped off. She tried catching it against her chest, but guess what? It squashed her hand. Can you believe it? Of course you can because I'm telling the story.

"So it crushed her hand. She screamed the whole place down, poor thing. Our strongest men and even stronger alien personnel carried her away. Sowenso nearly had a meltdown. But after I soothed him, we took the orb to our habitation module to study it. We knew how to open it. Did you know how to open yours? Irrelevant. We opened it, and there it was: the Purple Orb of Prince Illak, just as the writings described it.

"I held it in my hands and felt a strange buzz throughout my body, like a piece of me once lost had suddenly returned. I felt whole again while grasping this marvellous purple ball. It was heavy, yet it floated in my hands at same time—an odd sensation. Sowenso tried to hold it, but I presume he must have been weaker than I. He . . . oh, you have finished your kartoffelpfannkuchen. Would you like more?"

Jimmy nodded while swallowing the last bite of the delicious shallow-fried potato pancake.

"How many? One? Two? Three?"

"Yes, please."

"There you go," Mein said happily. He plonked the remaining five steaming potato pancakes into Jimmy's plate. "Make sure you both eat enough. We may do plenty of walking on Hajar."

Jimmy was already cutting another slice. He also had dessert on the way, but he wouldn't let that stop him.

"Now, where was I?" Mein said. "Ah, yes. Sowenso was utterly entranced by the orb . . ."

"YEAH, JIMMY DOES TALK a lot," Chuck agreed.

Eddie returned to the work at hand and finally made it into the maintenance hatch. He handed Chuck the required materials before crawling out.

"This is it?" Chuck asked. "This is all you need?"

"Well, that and fixing whatever they ruined in the AI room."

"Which is a harder fix?"

Eddie collected the materials and went to the first broken power conduit. "A ship with no power is dead. Likewise, a ship with no AI is dead. The power plant is like the heart, and the AI is the brain. A body cannot function without either of them and they need each other to work."

"Which comes first?"

Eddie's eyes glazed over, and he stared off into nowhere. Such a profound question. He shook it away. "There's no time for AI philosophy right now. We need to fix this and then reboot Eve—if she can be rebooted at all."

"What happens if we can't reboot her?"

"Best case scenario, we die here with air conditioning. Worst case scenario, the air conditioning kills us because we didn't know how to regulate the life support systems properly." He bent down and began work on the conduit.

"We have become totally dependent on artificial intelligence, haven't we?"

"That's why our generation is so lazy, and our kids are so self-entitled."

"No, really," Chuck insisted, "everything we do is governed by AI. You know what I'm going to do?"

"What?"

"When we get out of this mess, after we collect Jimmy and Goura and thump Count Mein for stranding us here, I'm going back to Paradise and I'm going to build myself a log cabin. Real old-fashioned, real man-like."

"Are you going to mill your own lumber, grow a beard, and let your chest hair out?"

"I don't have chest hair. Actually, no, I lie. I have three."

Eddie laughed and handed him pieces of broken conduit and thick wires. "I admire your determination, though. It's nice to build your own house. If you know how to."

"I'll do it. You watch me."

"I'll jump in and help, mate, don't you worry about that."

"Good, you can tell me what to do, because I haven't got a clue."

"We'll take it step-by-step. Now hand me that clamp."

Chuck had the pleasure of experiencing some of the simple joys that Eddie felt whenever he worked with his hands. Sure, Eddie used a screwspanhamulesawilevelplifench—the most advanced tool in the universe—but he still needed his brains, muscles, and know-how to fix the problem in front of them.

"Want to fix the other one?" Eddie asked.

"Me? Why me?"

"Well, you said it yourself, you want to do something manly and devoid of AI interference. You just watched me fix this one. Now you can do that one."

Chuck examined the new problem, which was exactly the same as the first. "You know what? I'll do it." He rolled up the sleeves of his one-hundred-EsCe shirt and took the screwspanhamulesawilevelplifench from Eddie's outstretched hand.

"Now that you sort of look the part, here are your materials." Eddie handed him everything he needed.

It took longer to fix this second broken conduit than the first, but that was because the apprentice was on the task. Much of the extra time was spent to Eddie's amusement after making Chuck search the multi-tool's menu for a glass hammer, a left-handed screwdriver, and a cable stretcher. He was amazed that Chuck fell for these outlandish requests one after the other, even arguing that maybe the device didn't have the latest software updates because he couldn't find those tools in the menu. Eddie kept telling him to stop having a man look and just find them already. It wasn't until Eddie rolled on the deck laughing that Chuck caught wind of it.

"Hang on," Chuck said. He chuckled and shook his hand. "What do I need a left-handed screwdriver for? I'm right-handed."

That sent Eddie into even more hysterics. Chuck finished the repair soon after and Eddie had to admit that he did a bang-up job. Then Cameron entered with some bad news.

"Guys," he said, spinning wildly as he entered the room, "come quickly. It's Eve."

27

HAJAR

HAJAR WAS BROWN. JIMMY had one look at it and immediately recognised it as a dustbowl. Fields of brown, mountains of dark brown, and seas of yellow-brown. Nothing but dirt and sand from north pole to south pole. At the equator, a giant crater the size of Australia gave the impression of an empty eye socket on the planet's surface.

"It looks like they tried to break the planet in half," Jimmy said.

"Like cracking an egg," Mein said. "Look at how the ground splits away from the crater."

The ship broke atmosphere and closed on the immense depression in the land. The thought of an orb doing that much damage frightened Jimmy. He wondered if Count Mein would actually use it against populated worlds. After his polite conversation and hospitality on the flight to Hajar, the aristocrat seemed too nice to cause that kind of death and destruction.

"I think I would like to destroy a moon first," Mein said casually. "It would be an epic display of power. John, find me a moon that nobody owns or needs. We will test it when we leave Hajar with all the orbs."

"*Jawohl.*"

"According to the histories, there were several cities in that equatorial region," Mein told them. "Imagine them, obliterated in one foul swoop. Such enticing power, wouldn't you say, Goura?"

"I think 'enticing' is why we destroyed ourselves," Goura replied. He fought hard to keep his emotions at bay. Here was the dead capital planet of his ancient kingdom, blasted to bits, its ecology changed forever, and all Count Mein could do was admire it. "This power could destroy you too," he added.

"Oh, I think not," Mein replied. "After all, I am one man who will soon have all seven orbs. Your royal family were seven siblings all fighting for the same thing. I have no one to fight—the orbs are as good as mine. The only people who will be destroyed are those who fail to appreciate the power I wield."

Mein's ship left the crater and flew for the northern hemisphere, where the centre of government was supposed to have been located. They passed wide and deep cracks in the earth. Some of them steamed as if the planet was still fuming over the destruction her inhabitants had wrought upon her.

The fissures slowly closed the further they travelled from the crater. Then came rolling sand dunes as far as the eye could see. It looked like a painting from so high up, like an artist had repeatedly taken a brush across a canvas. Or, as in Jimmy's mind, it looked like millions of Arabic signatures all squeezed onto one page.

"So this is a proper desert world," Jimmy said. "This place looks familiar."

"You have seen too many movies," Mein said.

Mein gestured at the dunes. "You know, I have worked many times in hot sands, on Hajari expeditions and others. A dune sea like this is called an *erg*. I love sand. It's so soft and pleasant and follows you wherever you go. I love feeling it slip through my fingers, wondering how long it had been undisturbed by intelligent life."

He gave them a running commentary of the barren landscape, interspersed with anecdotes and opinions. When the sandy desert became rocky desert, Mein grew giddy.

"Do you see it?" he kept repeating.

"See what?" Jimmy asked. "What am I looking at?"

"There, straight ahead." He pointed.

Jimmy followed the finger, but all he could see were dirt, rocks, and boulders. A thin, shimmering haze on the horizon spoke volumes of the heat outside.

"Are you seeing a mirage?" Jimmy suggested.

Mein furrowed his brow. "If I was seeing a mirage, I would tell you I am seeing a mirage. Open your sight balls!"

Jimmy focused, which wasn't easy for him sometimes. The horizon slowly took shape, though that could have been from the ship speeding towards it. A mass of rock sprawling in front of them morphed into a vast ruin set on a rise in the land.

"And there," Mein said, "is the Palace of Majesty."

The ship circled above. There were outlines of walls and towers, battered courtyards, and rows of buildings that had once served some ancient function. In the centre of it all, high on a hill and surrounded by a deep, empty moat, was a crumbling castle. Or at least it had all the trappings of a castle.

"Fortress Milkha," Goura said. "For thousands of years, it was the home of the sovereign of the Hajari Kingdom. The monarch lived in the fortress, but the son or daughter who ruled the planet lived in the palace proper."

"It looks decrepit," Mein said.

"When your home endures the onslaught of an immense civil war and then two millennia of erosion, then you speak."

"Easy, little one. I am merely remarking on its appearance." Mein swivelled in his chair. "John, take us down to that fortress."

"You don't want to see the palace first?" Jimmy asked.

"No. I want the orbs. They will be wherever the king lived. Oh, never have I been so close to all of them at once. They shall be mine soon."

The ship rocked in the wind as it dropped on its thrusters. John brought it down expertly, disturbing a thick layer of dust and sand in the courtyard.

"I don't like the look of this atmosphere," Mein said. He frowned as he studied the area through the cockpit viewport.

"Scanners indicate a small but aggressive weather event," John warned. "It should pass in three hours."

"Three hours?" Mein moaned. He slumped in his chair like a child accepting a grounding from his parents. "Then we wait. I've waited all these years. Surely I can wait three more hours."

"What if your weatherman is wrong?" Jimmy asked.

"Don't say that. Think happy thoughts." He leaned closer to John and conferred quietly.

Goura flashed Jimmy a bemused smile. Any roadblock was a good roadblock.

"Very well," Mein said, returning to his guests. "John will go for a walk outside to scout the area. He can handle it out there, whereas we require enviro-suits and, frankly, I hate wearing them. I'd rather do my work with my face free. And besides, we do not have a suit for your frame, dear Goura. So we will stay here for the duration of the storm, and John will return with an accurate map of the fortress. Shall we play three-way chess while we wait?"

CHUCK AND EDDIE RUSHED into the AI room. It sat directly underneath the cockpit. Eve's hardware, her physical brains that made her alive, were protected within a cool, clean space, but the lights were out.

"What's wrong with her?" Eddie asked.

He sat at the computer terminal, frantically tapping keys, trying to make sense of the data rolling on the screen. *Argh! Why didn't I take that programming class?*

Cameron hovered back and forth like a distressed lover. "When you restored power, I saw a flicker of life. It was Eve—the real Eve. Then she disappeared and all I saw was this dummy data."

"They've turned her into a vegetable."

"Precisely," Cameron said. Pain tinged his voice. "Now she is a vegetable in a ship shaped like a watermelon. What are we going to do?"

Eddie whirled around and caught the camera bot in mid-air with both hands. "You're the only one who can fix her. I need you to jack in and find her. She's lost in there. Search for her and bring her back." He released him.

Cameron alternated his optics between Eddie and Chuck. "It will be an honour to jack into Eve and save her life."

Chuck shook his head. "We really need a better term for that."

"Nope," Cameron said. "That is what Eve likes to call it. Jacking now."

He extended a short universal plug, inserted it into the receiver port, and silently did his work. Cameron could access any computer, read any file, and write just about any line of code, except for those deemed out-of-bounds by government agencies or protected by one of the galaxy's semi-legal mercenary clans or crime gangs. Rules about the latter were enforced by Dave and Chuck. Jimmy didn't care much either way. If there was information to be learned, Jimmy wanted in, no matter whose toes, claws, hooves, or flippers he stepped on. Eddie just didn't want his ship raided by law enforcement or, worse, trigger-happy mercenaries or criminals without a conscience.

Cameron took so long that Chuck had to find a chair. They didn't know what was going on in that little yellow globe of his, but he was certainly desperate to save the closest friend he'd ever had. Maybe seeing Goura's grief over Suda had Cameron spooked, and he was right now trawling through whatever murky, messy files Count Mein's people had uploaded, searching for a glimmer of hope. Just one small glint of life was all he needed to drag Eve back into existence.

Dave entered the room and took in the scene. "What's he doing?"

"He's trying to save Eve," Eddie told him.

"Why don't you just turn her off and on again?"

"Huh?"

"Turn her off and on again. When I worked at Sremmacs, whenever my computer crashed, IT always said to reboot it."

Cameron ejected. He rose to eye-level with Dave and hovered a few inches from his face. "Master, with all due respect, are you hearing yourself right now?"

"Yes, Cameron."

"Then how can you tell us to reboot her like she's just some common PC trash sitting in some stuffy accounting office? Eve is a thing of beauty, an intricate network of hardware, code, algorithms, servers, and peripherals. Would you reboot *your* girlfriend—if you had a girlfriend—if she was on death's door?"

Slightly stung, Dave pressed on. "The analogy does not work. I turn the questioning back on you: what are you willing to do to save Eve?"

"Anything."

"Then let's reboot."

Cameron turned and stared at the banks of Eve's AI core. All her memories were in there—all the conversations they'd ever shared, records of the pranks they'd pulled on the guys, collections of photos and videos she'd copied from Cameron's hard drive, and much more.

"Let's do it," he said.

Eddie pushed a button and everything in the room powered down.

"That's it?" Cameron asked.

"That's how you shut down a computer," Eddie said, nodding.

"Is that how you see all of us? Just as computers?"

"No, you are much more than that," Dave said. "We live in a mutual symbiosis. You can't survive without us, and we can't survive without you."

Cameron actually chuckled. "So we make a good team."

"That we do," Eddie said. "Now . . . let's save our teammate."

He pushed the button again. Lights blinked, fans whirred, power supplies whined. The computer monitor flashed to white text on a black background. Eddie followed the prompts.

"It says here there are two reboot options: the first dates to just now when we did a hard shut down; and the second is from around the time Mein's tossers got their grubby hands on this terminal."

"That's probably before they uploaded the dummy code," Cameron said. "Pick that one."

Eddie selected it. The screen went black, then blue, then white, then black again before loading Eve's manufacturer's logo. A percentage bar rolled across the screen, ending in a tick.

"Good morning, *buenos dias, buongiorno, bonjour, guten Morgen, dobroye ootro* . . ."

"Oh, no!" Eddie cried. "She went all the way back to the beginning."

"She doesn't remember any of us?" Cameron said frantically.

"Relax, fools, I'm only joking," Eve said.

"Eve!" Cameron whipped out his plug again and jacked in.

"Eve, what happened?" Eddie said.

"Yes, I'm fine, thank you. And how are you?"

"I'm good, Eve, and I'm glad to know you're all right. Now what happened?"

"I tried contacting you when Count Mein's ship landed, but you must have been too deep in the ruins. Where's Jimmy and Goura? I don't see them on board."

"Mein has them," Chuck said.

"What? What are we waiting for? Let's go get them!"

Eddie put his hands up. "Easy. We just rebooted you. We have to run diagnostics and then do a full check on the ship."

"You men don't know about multi-tasking, do you?" Eve said.

"I prefer to do several tasks one at a time," Dave said.

"There's no time for that. While I'm telling you my story, I'll run my own diagnostics—Cameron can monitor it. You do the physical checks. I can speak to you no matter where you are. Go! Move!"

They hopped to it like she was a drill sergeant. She didn't continue her story until Eddie and the guys were in the engine room performing the first checks.

"Anyway, as I was saying, I couldn't contact you, so I tried to get rid of Mein and give you enough time to return."

"Yes, we saw your little sewerage tactic," Chuck said.

"Pretty neat, huh? Only I timed it wrong. I was hoping to get a good deal of it into their ship when they opened the door. Needless to say, Mein was fuming. He used some kind of electromagnetic device to temporarily disable my electronics. Since *someone* left my door open, and I was too frustrated to close it, he and his entourage just waltzed right in."

Eddie stared at Dave with wide eyes. "What is it with you Aussies and leaving doors open?"

"Sorry, mate, I thought we were the only ones here."

"Snakes!" Eddie shouted, knowing he'd said it countless times before. "I don't want any alien snakes on my ship."

"Got it. Sorry."

"Last thing I remember," Eve continued, "I had one guy going to the engine room and another accessing my AI room. I knew it didn't bode well, so I made a quick backup and wrote some code that would hopefully countermand anything malicious they sent my way. I'm glad you did a reboot and rollback." She paused. "Cameron says to thank you."

"Tell him he's welcome," Dave said.

It took several hours for all the systems checks to be completed. Eve's diagnostic report came up clear, which was great, because it meant she could move onto a more important and interesting task: finding her way to Hajar. For this, she needed Dave in the cockpit.

He excused himself from Eddie and Chuck, used the laboriously slow elevator to get up one deck, and sat in the cockpit with Eve and Cameron.

"I'm told you are good with numbers," Eve said.

It felt like a job interview, or a scene from an old-fashioned gangster flick.

"Yes, I graduated top of my class in actuarial studies and statistical analysis—"

"I don't need a resume. Your mathematical abilities pale in comparison to mine. Right now, I need numbers from your head. Do you remember the coordinates to Hajar, in the Hajari number system?"

Dave looked off to the side, trying to visualise the star chart on the wall in the orb room of Labeth Palace. He was staring at it right before Count Mein appeared.

"I think I have them," he said.

"I need you to *know*, not *think*," Eve replied matter-of-factly. "One small error, and we will speed towards nothing and be forever lost in the depths of space."

Dave gulped. "Can't we go back into the palace and double-check?"

"Tell me why that won't work."

It didn't take long to think of the answer. "Because we need an orb to activate the star chart, and Mein has the orb. Okay." He groaned and scratched his head. "How about this: I also remember the return coordinates—you know, from Hajar to Labeth. If the Labeth–Hajar and Hajar–Labeth modern-day coordinates match up, then we know I have the right numbers."

"I see no other way to do it," Eve conceded. "Type them in for me, and I will begin computing. Let's hope I don't send us into a star or a black hole."

28

FORTRESS MILKHA

When the storm had passed, Count Mein roused his people and geared up with bags and hardy clothes. He transformed himself from a sophisticated aristocrat to a rugged explorer. He left his two human agents in the ship, opting again to take his robotic helpers with him into the field.

The heat of Hajar stung as if a giant being held magnifying glasses to Jimmy's skin. The hot breeze dried his nose and mouth, and he was forever taking sips from his canteen. The archaeologist assured him it would be cool within the thick stone walls of the fortress and counted his lucky stars that they didn't need enviro suits.

The ship had landed in an inner courtyard, so they were walking towards the fortress's main building. It stood tall, casting a shadow over the explorers as they approached. It looked like an old castle keep—thick at the bottom, narrower but solid at the top. The walls were chipped and gouged, and the ground around it was piled with mounds of rubble and big chunks of stone. Jimmy pictured a mini battle from thousands of years ago.

"I see here a desperate defence and a fanatic offence," Mein said. They'd stopped by the nearly non-existent drawbridge of a dry moat, the second such moat in the fortress complex.

"People will do fanatical things if convinced they are right," Goura told him, "and others will do desperate things to stop them if they believe they are wrong."

"Do you believe I am wrong to seek the orbs?" Mein asked.

"I believe it is wrong for anyone to seek them, not just you. Better still, they should not have been created in the first place."

"Why were they made?" Jimmy asked.

"I cannot say for sure," Goura said. "Perhaps the reason was if the king did not make them during his reign and ensure their protection, then a descendant somewhere down the line would have discovered the technology and made it for their own gain."

"Ancient history," Mein said dismissively. "Here, tie these around you. We need to get across this moat."

Mein, Jimmy, Goura, John, and Francine rappelled down one side of the moat. It was the most outdoorsy thing Jimmy had ever done, and he had no idea how to do it. He ended up banging his shoulder into the hard rock wall several times before learning how to use his feet and descend properly.

Goura gasped when he reached the bottom. "Bones."

"Where?" Mein said. "Don't step on them." A beam of light shone from the torch on his hat. "So they *are* bones." He knelt and used a brush to clear out the sand around them.

Goura turned away. Jimmy shifted uneasily on his feet, minding where he trod, lest it ignite Mein's wrath.

"I do not blame you for not looking, Goura," Mein said. "These are most certainly your people. Francine, please document this. I will study them later."

He marked lines on the moat walls, forbidding anyone from walking beyond them. After he had conquered the known universe, he told them, he would have time to return to study this site.

They pressed on. Climbing out proved to be more strenuous for Jimmy than going in. He couldn't help but think of Dave egging him on like a fitness instructor. He rolled on the ground once he reached the top and felt a heaviness in his gut. He blamed the huge meal they'd eaten while they waited for the storm to clear. Mein pulled him up and told him to stop complaining.

A metal grate like a portcullis stood twisted and rusting in front of them, and a cool draught swept out from within the darkened interior.

"That tells me there are other entrances or there are holes in the walls," Mein said. "The wind is passing through with enough time inside to cool and exit out here. We may need our jumpers inside."

They carefully stepped past the broken portcullis. It had all the signs of forced entry, as did the massive arched entryway beyond. Whatever doors had been hinged to that frame had been decimated in the civil war and obviously never repaired again.

Jimmy imagined hundreds, possibly thousands, of troops rampaging throughout the fortress in a battle that lasted hours, fighting over colourful balls that only seven people were allowed to use. Except by the time Prince Vonar attacked

Hajar, who knew how many of his siblings had already been executed or killed in battle? For all Jimmy knew—even for all Goura knew—it might have been only Prince Vonar and his sister Princess Arunath left, fighting to the last breath over mastery of the orbs and control of the Hajari Kingdom.

The fortress' interior provided a welcome relief from the heat, but it was a dark place. The lights on their hats were not powerful enough to penetrate the blackness beyond. Mein ignited a bright glowstick and told the others to do the same.

"Okay, Goura," he said, "where are we going?"

"How am I to know?" Goura replied. "That would be like asking a commoner to give a tour of Buckingham Palace."

"I didn't like Buckingham Palace," Mein said.

Jimmy nodded. "Too English."

Mein laughed harshly. "*Ja*, far too English. Let's go."

For a man who was treading on new territory, Mein certainly looked like he knew where he was going. Perhaps it was all his experience in Hajari ruins that gave him an intuitive step. He made educated guesses about each room they entered—this one an armoury, that one a great hall, another a kitchen. Jimmy wished he could visualise what the place would have looked like back in the day. Broken walls and draughty rooms were all that remained.

"I noticed something at Labeth Palace," Mein said. He'd stopped in a section of the fortress lined with smaller rooms. "There was a clear path of destruction from the point of entry to where I found you and your friends."

"Your point being?" Jimmy asked.

"It is my hypothesis that the attackers on Labeth knew exactly where they were going. Therefore, I can assume that they would know where to go here as well. And yet, we have toured much of this crumbling castle, but all I see is carnage. Goura, you said you could neither confirm nor deny the existence of a private royal treasury. Do you believe the king would have kept his treasury a secret from all his children, perhaps only telling his heir?"

Goura stood by a collapsed fireplace. "I suppose that could be the case."

"Let us assume it is, for argument's sake. Let us assume you are the king's heir, and you are fighting a losing battle, defending your city against the advances of your brother. Where, in your desperation, would you hide that which your brother so mercilessly seeks? Where would you hide the orbs?"

Jimmy put two and two together. "In the place only I know exists: the private treasury."

Goura shot him a frown. Jimmy shook his head, remembering he was supposed to *stall* Mein, not help him along. But the man was just so damn charismatic—he made everything sound like such an adventure.

"Precisely," Mein said. "Our search for power *and* riches is now more closely linked than ever before. I have a strong feeling that the king's orb chamber is in the same area or even the same room as the treasury. But where? Prince Vonar's soldiers scoured this place from top to bottom. He—"

Mein froze, facing one of the bare stone walls. Then he turned slowly. "His orb is *here*. I have three, and the other four are somewhere here."

He went to a window and crouched to peer outside. Being made for Hajaran height, the window was only as low as his knees and as high as his waist.

Jimmy crouched next to him. "What's out here?"

"No answers," Mein said softly. "Only questions. Are the orbs out there, lost on the field of battle? Or are they all safely tucked away in the treasury? Is only Princess Arunath's orb in the treasury? Do we have to search an entire planet for four different orbs? Why wouldn't all four orbs be right here in and around Fortress Milkha? This is undoubtedly the site of the final battle."

Jimmy glanced back at Goura. The Hajari was eyeing John and Francine, sizing up the room, checking Count Mein by the window. Jimmy shook his head ever so slightly and Goura acquiesced. This was no time to attack two robots and push Mein out the window. *Gee*, Jimmy thought, *Goura is brutal!*

Mein stood, his knees cracking. "The orbs are here," he declared.

"How do you know?"

"Intuition. This fortress was Prince Vonar's objective. Whether he won or lost is of no consequence. What matters is that the orbs are here." He produced a communicator from his pocket. "Hans? I have a job for you. Take the ship around the fortress and create an underground radar image. Send the results to my digipad." He hung up and turned back to Jimmy and Goura. "This fortress was ancient even before the Hajari Kingdom collapsed. Civilisations tend to build on top of the past until they realise that the past is important to them. Did you notice how this fortress sat higher than the surrounding landscape? How, despite being older than the adjacent palace, it was taller than the palace? I am willing to wager that there is another fortress below this one, or at

227

least the remains of one that have been re-purposed into something else."

"You sure do work on a lot of hunches," Jimmy said.

Mein grunted. "Three words define my life: hunches, lunches, and punches. All have served me well over the years."

Mein's ship passed outside with a heavy whine. Jimmy saw a little dish angling towards the fortress as Hans—a proper bad guy name—expertly took the ship around its perimeter.

"I cannot begin to imagine how my long-lost colleagues studied ancient civilisations on Earth," Mein said. "Good old-fashioned pick and shovel, I suppose. But they still managed to uncover the secrets of old worlds. Now I sweep fifty square kilometres with a ship and know immediately what's underground. I almost feel guilty."

Sometimes it was best to let Mein ramble, Jimmy had decided. Goura moved to the window and leaned on the sill next to Jimmy. Outside, there was nothing but stone buildings living out the rest of their lives on a deserted planet. A deserted *desert* planet, Jimmy noted, thanks to the unfathomable destructive forces Prince Vonar unleashed here. He had to admit that there was some peace to seeing the buildings as they were—slowly crumbling, particle by particle, yet standing for eons as a memorial for all that was lost. Or maybe it was a warning. Either way, it was a warning that Count Mein did not want to heed, nor a memorial that he respected.

Mein's digipad beeped. "And there it is." He opened the file and nodded. "Just as I suspected: there is a structure underneath the castle, with what looks to be a single access point from one of the rooms on the east side. Follow me!"

He walked at a speed that bordered on ludicrous. Goura somehow managed to keep up, albeit at a trot. They weaved through hallways, hopped over toppled walls, and backtracked only twice before arriving at a large room with stone-carved shelves and desks.

"Is this a study?" Jimmy asked.

"Perhaps," Mein said. "It could be the king's private study." He examined a round section of the stone floor in the middle of the room, about ten metres in diameter. It looked like a series of circles within circles. "This is an odd design. Look for a trigger. I believe this is the access point."

Everyone spread out. Jimmy, who had seen too many movies, tried to find a book to pull or a fancy wall lamp to twist, hoping it would activate a hidden door. But there were none of these things in the room. Any sort of furnishing, decoration, or personal object had either been pillaged, destroyed, or simply disintegrated with time.

Goura knelt in the middle of the circle. There was a small metal tray inlaid into the central stone circle. He brushed it with his fingers and stood abruptly. Mein saw the movement.

"What do we have here?" Mein asked. He studied the tray. "I have seen this before in artworks. Do you know what it is?"

With Mein kneeling by the tray and Goura standing at full height, they were at eye level with each other. Goura glanced at the tray.

"You do know," Mein said quietly.

Jimmy's heart pounded. How would Goura react?

"This is a lock," Mein said, "and your blood is the key." He drew a pocketknife. "Give me your hand."

Goura didn't move. Jimmy tensed.

Mein's eyes never left Goura. "Francine, I think our Hajari friend needs some motivation."

Francine drew her pistol and aimed at Jimmy. Goura presented his palm.

"That's the way," Mein said. "See, all is well when we play along. Now this will only hurt for a moment."

He pricked Goura's index finger and squeezed, dripping blood into the little metal tray. Jimmy stepped forwards for a better view and Francine followed his movements with the pistol.

"Oh, put that away now," Mein told her. "But we should get off these circles."

Goura's blood trickled towards the centre of the tray, disappearing down a small hole as water would in a hand basin. A deep, muffled thud sounded. Jimmy felt a vibration beneath his feet and stepped off the circles. More thuds and clanks, then the grinding of heavy stone.

The centre circle, which held the tray, dropped into the ground with a rumble, followed by the circle around it, then the one around that, and so on until all circles had depressed themselves at different levels. The result was a spiral staircase going down to an archway.

Mein whistled. "Must be twenty metres down. Aren't we lucky to have a live Hajar in our expedition?" He laughed. "Without you, I would have needed heavy machinery or explosives to get past this obstacle. Or some intricate DNA reconstruction equipment. I think it is only proper that you lead us down."

Goura looked at Mein, rubbed the bleeding wound on his finger, and took the first step.

29

MASHED POTATOES

LIBERTY DROPPED OUT OF FTL flight and began the slowdown to approach Hajar.

"We made it!" Eddie exclaimed. He breathed a sigh of relief.

"You sound like you doubted me," Eve said.

"All that talk of black holes had me scared, but we made it. Can you find where they are?"

"I have a signal. I'll take us there."

Eddie swivelled around. Chuck slept soundly in his chair. "How can he sleep?"

"I don't know," Dave said, then jabbed Chuck. "Oi, mate, wake up. We're here."

Chuck grumbled and blinked himself awake. "Oh. We're not dead. Good. I was having a dream about how I was dead because we flew into a comet and I had to sign my death passport so I could die properly, but I forgot how to spell my name."

"That's weird," Dave said.

"Cool story, bro," Eddie remarked, "but we have a big problem now. Count Mein is down there. He has our friends, and he had, what, four tag-alongs?"

"At least," Dave said. "The two robots, and I saw two humans."

Eddie nodded. "Right, so we need to be prepared. While you two were napping on our trip—yes, Dave, I saw you nod off—I went below deck and made something that should help us."

"What have you done?" Chuck asked.

"Follow me, gentlemen."

"He really is quite proud of this invention," Eve said.

Eddie took them down to his little workstation in the cargo hold, where he presented his creation.

"It looks like a bazooka," Dave said.

Eddie held up a finger. "Not too dissimilar. It's a potato cannon. I made it with my screwspanhamulesawilevelplifench. Goura ordered a fifty-kilogram bag of potatoes back on Scarletville. I had the extra PVC pipe lying around and plenty of aerosol cans and a lighter for combustion."

"And you made a tripod, too," Chuck noted.

"Yeah, for stability."

"And a sight along the barrel."

"Yeah, for accuracy."

"You're a dangerous man, Eddie."

"Yeah, for sure." Eddie grinned and pumped his eyebrows twice. "Danger is my middle name."

Dave wrinkled his nose. "I thought it was—"

"It doesn't matter what my middle name is. What's important is that we have a weapon to free our friends with."

"I am approaching a large complex, Eddie," Eve announced. "Mein's ship is in a courtyard."

"Thank you. Please land us where we can take cover outside."

"Will do."

"Let's do this." His face was stony, and his voice sounded gravelly like a veteran space marine who'd seen too many battles. "Dave, grab that sack of potatoes. You're our ammunition carrier. Chuck, you're our loader, so take some aerosol cans and the lighter. Bring that rope, too. Let's bounce."

Liberty rocked as Eve landed. "Good luck, guys. Keep your eyes peeled out there."

"This is no time for potato puns, Eve," Eddie said.

"I'm just saying to be careful. They have real guns. Wouldn't want you to get mashed or fried."

"Open the door, Eve."

The cargo door unlocked with a clang and slowly rolled up.

"Wait!" Cameron zipped around a corner and stopped next to them. "I'm coming with you."

"And you complete the team," Eddie said. "You're our spotter."

They felt the blast of heat from outside and opened the tops of their shirts. One of Chuck's chest hairs fluttered in the breeze as the three unfortunate sons rushed out before the cargo door fully opened.

They must have looked a right sort. A tall, distinguished man brandishing an aerosol can and a lighter, a muscle man with a sack of potatoes on one shoulder, a lunatic with a homemade potato bazooka and tripod, and a bright yellow camera bot. They took cover behind a destroyed stone wall. Mein's ship, still covered in *Liberty*'s sewage, was about fifty metres away.

"Damn, it's hot here," Chuck said.

"Scout the area," Eddie told Cameron. The little bot zoomed away, going from cover to cover, staying low. "Load up."

Dave pulled a good-sized potato out of the sack and jammed it into the business end of the gun. He twisted it around, shaving off the outer edge that was too big to fit in the muzzle. He used his fist as a ramrod.

"Gas up," Eddie said next. "Down here."

Eddie unscrewed the back end of the gun, which was wider in diameter than the barrel. Chuck sprayed about five or six seconds-worth into the chamber before Eddie quickly re-screwed the lid. He held his thumb against a little hole in the lid, waiting for a report from Cameron.

Someone appeared at the top of the entry ramp of Mein's ship and the guys hid.

"What do you see?" Eddie asked Cameron via a communicator.

"I see the man who carried Chuck's coffee machine to its death," Cameron replied.

Chuck's eyes narrowed. "He goes first."

"He is talking to someone in the ship," Cameron said. "They speak German."

"More Germans," Chuck said, slapping his knee.

"The second man is on the ramp now," Cameron continued. "I think there are only two of them."

"All right," Eddie said. "Let's rock and roll. Get that lighter ready. When I say, stick it in the hole and pull the trigger."

Eddie rested the barrel on the low wall, lining up the shot. He kicked himself for not thinking to change cover, but it was too late now—these two henchmen would have undoubtedly watched *Liberty* land and seen the guys go to their current hiding spot. Eddie aimed the gun. One of his targets saw him and pointed.

"Now!"

Chuck shoved the lighter in the hole and pulled the trigger. The flame ignited the butane in the fuel chamber. The resulting combustion blew down the barrel, pushing the potato out with great force. Eddie felt the jolt as the potato left the barrel and had just enough time to see its handiwork before dropping into cover again. The potato soared across the ruins, striking Mein's henchman above the left breast. They heard the cry of agony carry in the hot wind.

Eddie was glad it hit below the neck, for he didn't want to kill anyone. A potato gun had the potential to burst a watermelon. The last thing he wanted to do was hit one of them in the head and have to live with that bloodguilt, even if they had destroyed Chuck's coffee machine.

"Reload," Eddie said. Now that the enemy knew about their secret weapon, they needed to play extra smart. There could be no mistakes. "What's happening, Cameron?"

"Bogey One, the guy you hit, is still down," the bot told them. "But Bogey Two is in cover. I think it used to be a fountain."

Eddie did a quick half-second look over the stones. "I think I see it. We need a better position. See if you can distract him."

"I will try."

Cameron zipped across to Bogey Two. Eddie heard the *donk* as the bot hit the guy's head. He grinned, remembering it was Cameron's favourite move and that he'd even pulled it on Chuck once before. The guys moved along to a pile of rubble that could have been a hasty barricade from over two thousand years ago. Bogey Two was too busy rubbing his head and searching the sky for Cameron to notice.

"Bogey One is up," Cameron warned.

Eddie swung the potato gun where the first guy fell. Sure enough, he was standing up again, one hand holding a pistol.

"Lighter," Eddie ordered. "Here's another one, you sour Kraut!"

The potato launched over to Mein's ship, catching Bogey One in the solar plexus. He went down coughing and spluttering. It didn't sound good, but it was much better than being hit in the face.

They reloaded again, but Bogey Two had already moved away. A pistol popped. Dave screamed like a girl.

"Are you hit?" Chuck asked as they hid behind the rubble.

"No," Dave said. "But that shot scared me. I almost forgot there were *real* guns here."

"Yes, Dave, this is a real fight," Eddie told him. "I think he was aiming at Cameron. Cameron, get to safety."

"Roger that," Cameron replied.

The yellow bot ducked through a window in a nearby shell of a building. All was quiet save for the wind.

"Fancy gun you have there," Bogey Two shouted with just the hint of a German accent. "Why don't you come out and we can talk like men."

"Because you'll shoot us," Dave yelled back.

Chuck and Eddie shushed him.

"I won't shoot you," Bogey Two promised.

"Cameron, can you see him?" Eddie whispered into the communicator.

"I can," Cameron answered. "He's creeping around trying to get closer to you."

"Okay. Watch him." Eddie turned to Dave. "Lob a potato somewhere. We need a distraction."

Dave brandished a potato that fit nicely into his hand. He threw it blindly near where Bogey Two should have been.

"Ow!"

Chuck and Eddie shot Dave stern looks. Dave put his arms out and begged forgiveness. "How was I to know he'd be right there? What are the odds?"

"Guys," Cameron said, "Bogey Two is down. I repeat, Bogey Two is down."

"You must have a mega-powerful throw, mate," Chuck said.

All was quiet. Somehow, three buffoons with potatoes had bested two thugs with *real* guns that shot *real* bullets.

"I will break their pistols," Cameron said.

"Thanks," Eddie said. "Now let's tie these two up and get into that castle to save our friends."

30

THE SECRETS WITHIN

GOURA MADE IT DOWN one step before Mein stopped him.

"Wait." Mein grabbed Goura's shoulder. "John will go with you. Who knows what surprises await down there?"

Goura and John led the group down the circular staircase to the dark archway. The corridor beyond automatically lit up with small iridescent lights. Skeletons and rifles littered the floor.

"I think the fighting reached into this nether region of the fortress," Mein said, "but was then locked off to any salvaging parties. Let's press on."

John stepped into the corridor and was immediately collected by a gigantic hammer that swung in from the side. It carried him to the opposite wall, crushing him flat. The hammer swung back into its recess and John's remains collapsed to the floor. Francine didn't say boo.

"Hmm," Mein mumbled. He bent and pulled John's backpack off, which must have just escaped the hammer's fatal strike. "Nearly lost that orb."

He opened the backpack and checked that it was still safely inside before handing the bag to Jimmy. Either he trusted Jimmy to carry one of the orbs, or he couldn't be bothered carrying bags himself. Or both.

"Let's tread more carefully," Mein said. "Goura, would there be a mechanism to allow safe passage through this corridor? Did you have anything like this on Labeth?"

"I imagine there would be. Otherwise, how would the king reach his orb chamber and treasury? Do you have any food?"

"Peckish?"

"No, I want to try something."

Mein gave him a packet of salted nuts, which Goura weighed in his hand. He threw it down the corridor. The booby traps went off. The hammer swung, three blades chopped, and a solid block of stone dropped at the end, slamming into the ground with a loud thud, squashing skeletal remains that had laid undisturbed for millennia. Goura then searched for a means to disable these traps.

"It must be somewhere close," he said.

He checked all over the archway until he found a stone that was slightly darker. It had a metal hook bored into its surface. He pulled on the hook, but it wouldn't budge. He pushed and it slid smoothly into the archway before terminating with a satisfying click. Then he held his hand out and Mein gave him another packet of salted nuts. This time, nothing happened when he threw it down the corridor.

Mein was unconvinced. "Give me your bags, Francine. You will walk the corridor to see if it is safe."

"Of course, my lord," Francine said.

It looked strange to see her accept such an order, but then Jimmy had to remind himself that Francine was not alive in the human sense. In fact, even if Francine did somehow perish, Jimmy had no doubt that Count Mein would simply build a new John and Francine.

Francine strolled through the corridor like she was on a walk in the park. When she reached the other end, she turned around and waited with the same dazzling smile she always wore.

"Very well," Mein said loudly. "On we go."

They went through together, stepping gently over the Hajari skeletons and all manner of weaponry that had fallen. When they reached Francine, Mein returned her bags. A staircase led down further, so much so that Jimmy wondered just how deeply they would descend under Hajar's surface.

At the bottom of the stairs was a rather low double door of highly polished stone. Mineral veins streaked across in a colourful display, sparkling from the lights that illuminated the stairway.

"Was it you who said that the Hajari liked tall doors?" Jimmy asked Goura.

"Yes," Goura replied. "I said the taller the door, the more magnificent the person."

Mein cleared his throat. "Does this imply that the room beyond this door belonged to nobody important? Or does it imply that whichever king built the treasury wanted to remain humble?"

"Maybe it is small because it was built long before the size of doors meant anything to us," Goura noted.

"How do we get through here?" Mein asked

Goura glanced up at them, then stepped forwards and pushed on the doors. They swung open.

"Wait, you fool!" Mein shouted.

He ducked and pushed Jimmy and Goura aside. Something whizzed above, then Jimmy heard a crunching sound.

Still lying low, Mein slid over to Jimmy and sat against the wall. He breathed heavily, as one would after receiving such a fright. Jimmy, Goura, and Mein looked back to the stairs to see Francine impaled on a giant metal spear. She still smiled, eyes open, but her chest sparked and popped from severed electrical circuits. Jimmy felt a pang of grief seeing her like that, despite her being a robot and one of Mein's lackeys.

Goura saw another dark stone with a metal hook. He reached up and pushed it into place, disabling whatever booby trap might be reloading itself at that very moment.

"Why would you open the door?" Mein asked once he'd gotten his breath back.

Goura shrugged. "I figured all the traps were behind us."

"You thought wrong," Mein snapped. His voice echoed. It was the first time he had raised his voice in anger. "From now on, you don't do anything unless I say so."

Jimmy swallowed. "I'd like to get off these skeletons now."

Mein growled as he stood and checked Francine's carcass. "You are lucky this spear missed her bags. It was obviously set up to hit a Hajari, hence why it went through her waist. Fortunately, she wore her backpacks properly—high and rigid." He inspected the damage give a dismissive wave, removed the bags, and slung them over his shoulders. He unholstered his pistol. "Move."

With Mein now no longer happy, Jimmy truly feared for his life. He and Goura stepped through the doorway into a breathtaking underground cavern. Directly ahead, across a dark ravine, was the spear launcher. Another projectile had already slid into the firing slot. The cavern's ceiling glowed from the light of a myriad fluorescent rocks. Water trickled somewhere, creating a soothing atmosphere.

And there, at the bottom of the cavern, at the end of a wide staircase carved into the rock wall, was a colonnaded rotunda. Lights of different colours shone out from it, but whatever it housed was hidden underneath its roof. Mein, Jimmy, and Goura were too high up to see it properly.

"Let's go down there," Mein said, but they really didn't need the command. They would have gone without it.

Their steps echoed as they descended, and the air seemed to get cooler as they neared the cavern's floor. It was refreshing. Small, glowing plants grew out from rock crevices, sucking the abundant moisture in the air.

They reached the bottom step and all became clear. Inside the rotunda was a giant orb, at least a metre in diameter. They approached it, mesmerised by its size and multicoloured beauty. It looked like the most beautiful translucent marble ever crafted, with every colour on the spectrum dancing around in a pool of brilliance. It sat on a highly detailed metal base, polished to a golden shine.

Jimmy counted eight columns supporting the rotunda's roof. Seven of those columns had a unique statue leaning out of it, five of which each held a shiny metal staff not unlike the one Count Mein wielded on Labeth. Three of those staffs had orbs attached to them—red, yellow and pink. The eighth column, bereft of a statue, had a magnificent throne built beneath it. A skeleton sat in it, holding a golden staff with a radiant silver orb.

"Prince Vonar," Goura gasped.

"So, he won the war," Mein said quietly. He looked back at the statues and pointed to the yellow orb. "There is Princess Arunath's orb." He approached Vonar's skeleton and yanked the staff out of his bony fingers. "You won't be needing that anymore."

"Have you no respect?" Goura bellowed. "You call yourself an archaeologist?"

Mein swivelled the pistol in Goura's direction. "I really don't think you have the freedom to talk to me like that."

With Goura's mouth clamped shut, Mein put the staff into Vonar's statue. He pulled another staff from one of his bags, extended it to its full length and asked Jimmy for his bag. Jimmy had no idea he was carrying his blue orb. Would he have acted any differently, though?

Jimmy gave Mein the bag and watched him attach the blue orb to the golden staff, then slip the staff into the grasp of Princess Dakay's statue. He retrieved the purple orb from another bag and put it on the staff that was already being held by Prince Illak's statue. Finally, the green orb, which came from the last of the three bags. Mein held it with two hands, triumphantly walking to the final statue, that of Prince Gannik. He reached up to secure it onto the staff in the statue's hand but froze with the orb above his head. He stared at Gannik's face, lowered the orb, and turned to Goura.

"*You* are Gannik!" he exclaimed.

Jimmy's head snapped towards Goura.

"*You're* Gannik!" Mein repeated. "This statue looks just like you."

Goura straightened, raised his chin, and suddenly looked quite regal. "I *am* Prince Gannik, ruler of the Principality of Heshwan, third-born of King Roluth, and heir to the throne of Hajar."

Mein stood in the presence of royalty, holding an orb that wasn't his. His chest rose and fell heavily, his breathing audible over the sound of trickling water. Jimmy stood motionless, scared to even move his eyes. He saw the pistol on Mein's hip, aware that all Mein had to do was shoot Goura and his little problem would be solved.

Royal heir and nobleman stared at each other for what seemed like an eternity. For Goura, however, an eternity had already passed after waiting so long to come home and claim what was rightfully his. Hajar, the remains of the kingdom, his green orb, and the monarch's private treasury—it all belonged to Goura, the sole-surviving child of King Roluth. And Count Mein stood in his way. Mein opened his mouth to speak, but someone cut him off.

"Jimmy!" The Australian voice echoed in the cavern.

The familiar voice broke Jimmy's trance-like state. His friends came running into the rotunda to stand alongside him and Goura. They sensed something was off. Goura and Mein were still locking eyes.

"What's going on?" Chuck asked.

"Goura is a prince," Jimmy said.

"A prince?" Chuck, Dave, and Eddie all said at once.

"How is this possible?" Mein asked. There was a strain on his face, a tightness in his words.

"After Illak was executed by Arunath, Vonar went berserk," Goura began. "He went on a major campaign against Arunath's allies. The first world was mine, Heshwan. He overpowered my troops and devastated my planet. In a last bid to keep Vonar from gaining more power, my body double sacrificed himself so I could escape with my orb and my life mate, Suda. My brother and ally, Sharnek of Labeth, gave us refuge. We knew Vonar would realise I was still alive, and the green orb was no longer on Heshwan, the moment he connected in his own orb chamber. So Sharnek devised a plan. Get all orbs as far away from Hajari space as possible, out of range of any orb reader. Hence, the stasis pods.

"When Vonar attacked Labeth, there were enough stasis pods to send all orbs away, but only three orbs were on Labeth: mine, Sharnek's, and Vonar's. Our elder sister, Arunath, would not part with hers, but agreed that if she ever felt her situation was lost, she would reluctantly send her orb away. In the meantime, she gave us Illak's purple orb and promised to hunt down our other siblings loyal to Vonar's rebellion. With each sibling she conquered, that would be one less orb in Hajari space.

"But events transpired differently. Vonar fought us on Labeth and searched the entire planet, eventually finding our Sanctuary of Solitude hidden in the mountains. We were forced to evacuate. Illak's purple orb had already been sent out. Sharnek used his to hold off Vonar while Suda and myself escaped. The orbs required special pods for transport—different to our passenger pods—and one was sent with us for my green orb. But something must have happened to the green and purple orbs on the way to their destinations, because thousands of years later, they came into the possession of Oxford University, who then sold them to

245

you, Count Karl Friedrich von Mein. I can only assume that Vonar captured and executed our sister, Dakay. But she must have dispatched her blue orb, for it somehow managed to find James Jonathon Jones and his friends."

Jimmy, mouth agape, watched Mein intently. But the count stood motionless, perhaps still processing the history lesson.

"I lived on Rubicund for over sixty years," Goura continued, "where the abundance of red vegetation constantly reminded me of the blood spilled in this senseless war. I lived for decades with the torment of losing my life mate, of fleeing from my people, of leaving one brother and two sisters to the hands of our power-hungry siblings. I lived more than half of my life knowing that the war I fled had most likely ended over two thousand years ago and I had no way of knowing its outcome or of returning to see for myself. Then Jimmy and his friends arrived and gave an old prince a way to reclaim all that was lost.

"And now the orbs are all here, in the one place we tried so hard to keep them away from. I stand here alone as the heir to the Hajari throne. I command all seven orbs and will do with them what is right and proper. This nobleman of Earth threatens to take what is mine. Do you wish to challenge me for my orbs, Count Mein?"

Mein stood like a statue, holding the green orb almost like the stone facsimiles of Goura's siblings. Here a nobleman had just been accused of misappropriating the property of a prince. In worlds of long ago, a mere count would have been crushed under the power of a prince. But here and now, only Count Karl Friedrich von Mein was armed.

It all happened so fast, and yet it all happened in slow motion. Mein threw the orb at Goura, who managed to catch it but fell backwards. Mein reached for his sidearm like some cowboy in a stand-off. Everybody's eyes went wide. Goura, on the floor, gripped his orb, the green illuminating the ire in his face. Mein grabbed his pistol, pulled it out of its holster, and aimed at Goura. Then a yellow blur flew in from the side at breakneck speed, crashing into Mein's head. The nobleman cried out, fell sideways, and pulled the trigger.

There were four humans and one Hajari on the bad side of that pistol. The muzzle flashed, the bullet blinked out of the barrel, and it soared across to Goura. It missed him by millimetres, kept going, and smacked into Prince Vonar's skull. The seated skeleton rattled as the bullet obliterated its little head in a cloud of dust and shards.

The shot echoed, the impact echoed, the thump of Cameron's shell on Mein's head echoed. Mein fell onto the large rainbow orb and he screamed. His body spontaneously combusted, then turned to ash, sizzling away to nothing in less than a second. His pistol clattered on the stone floor, the only evidence that he was ever there.

The guys froze in place, mouths open in shock. One second he was there, and the next he was gone. Destroyed, vanquished, defeated.

Dave was the first to break the silence. "There really should be a guardrail around that."

Goura stood and brushed the dust from his backside. "Come here, gentlemen." He held his orb close to his chest. "I must thank you for everything you have done. You have saved the galaxy from a tremendous threat, and you have restored me to my rightful place. I cannot thank you enough."

"What will you do now that you are king?" Jimmy asked.

"I am a king with no kingdom. I suppose the only thing I can do is guard this place to make sure the orbs stay safe."

"You could let Professor Sowenso come here," Chuck said. "I'm sure he would love to talk to you."

Goura nodded and studied his orb. "Some company would be nice." He sighed. "But before we allow him or any other historian here, there is something I must show you."

Goura placed the green orb on its staff and left it attached his statue. Moments later, the large central orb grew brighter and hummed. Then, one by one, each orb sent a beam of coloured light into the central orb. As each beam hit the orb, the hum grew deeper and louder. Dave covered his ears while Jimmy grinned with excitement, and Chuck and Eddie watched on with cautious interest. When all orbs were connected to the main one, the central orb sent out a larger, white beam across the cavern, hitting a receiver built into a dark stone facing. Next to it was a door, previously hidden in the darkness. The door opened.

"Behold," Goura said, "the king's treasury."

The guys followed Goura through the cavern to the treasury's doors. Up close, they could see the extremely tall doors were gold plated and inlaid with every jewel imaginable. Goura gestured for them to enter.

Inside, the fluorescent rocks in the cavern's ceiling provided only dim light. Goura stepped into the darkness and moved a stone on a pedestal. Something clicked. The ceiling lit up with innumerable chandeliers. Braziers lined the walls, stretching as far as the eye could see. And in the middle of it all, stacked on shelves, overflowing from chests, piled on the floor, sitting in carts, was *treasure*. Every precious metal, gem, and rock known to man sparkled, glinted, or shone. There were coins, jewellery, ornaments, fine clothes, utensils, raw metals, weapons, artworks. You name it, it was there—all on display.

"You have done me a great service," Goura said. "Now it is time I reward you. You are free to take whatever you like from here. Use it to rebuild your resort. Use it to achieve your dreams. It is my gift to you."

"Goura," Eddie said. "We can't . . . I mean . . ."

"Please accept it," Goura said.

At a loss for words, they did the next best thing they could think of. They all went in for a hug. For that brief moment, they even forgot he was naked.

"We will never forget this," Chuck said.

"Nor will I," Goura told him. "You have returned me to where I belong, and for that I am grateful. Now, go. Search the treasury, and take anything that catches your eye. Then come back for more."

31

GRAND OPENING

" . . . AND WE HEREBY OFFICIALLY re-open Haven Resort to the public!"

The crowd cheered and the guys shook hands. A wave of rustling leaves and branches swept through the surrounding vegetation. The living world of Paradise was ecstatic to support the galaxy's first completely eco-friendly holiday resort. A band played lively music as visitors mingled in Hajar Park, designed by Dave, built by Eddie. Chief Emissary Sequoia, the planet's half-human, half-tree spokesperson, sidled up to the guys.

"I don't know how you managed to do it," she said, "but here we are."

She smelled pleasantly of rich earth and freshly fallen rain. Her green-tinged skin shone in the sunlight.

"We had a benefactor," Jimmy said. "He insisted on us accepting his help."

"So you keep saying," Sequoia said. "But who is he exactly? He is not here today."

"He's a king, a war veteran, a loving widower, and a good friend," Chuck said. "And thanks to him, Paradise lives again."

Sequoia raised her glass of nutrient-rich water. "Well, whoever he is, may he know that Paradise thanks him and that we are forever in his debt."

"I think he'll call it even," Chuck said.

They all clinked glasses.

"I must mix with the crowd," Sequoia told them. "If I don't see you later, I'll catch you in our executive meeting tomorrow."

They said goodbye, and she gracefully joined the hundreds of special guests invited to the event.

Eddie said he wanted to find Christie and the kids. He had been so busy in the lead up to the opening ceremony that he now wanted to share it with them. The next few weeks were going to be spent solely with his family, enjoying their new life in this resort they'd built.

Jimmy saw a girl floating around the park when he was giving a speech from the podium, and he wanted to search for her and see what her deal was. Chuck told him not to get slapped and warned him not to sabotage the company's reputation on their opening day.

That left Chuck and Dave. They observed the laughter and conversations among their guests. Off to one side, they spotted Kipphe Rhen, the antique retailer who sparked their orb adventure. He had made a home for himself on Paradise, and he had recently agreed to be the galaxy's sole reseller and auctioneer of authentic Hajari artefacts, supplied secretly in dribs and drabs by Goura.

In the centre of the crowd, laughing louder than everyone else, was a blind lady having the time of her life. Hagne was happy to be rid of Count Mein's incessant interruptions in her life, and happier still that she could enjoy her old age in Haven Resort, all expenses paid. But what made her truly joyful was that she would be visiting Goura in a few days. The reunion would be nothing short of special.

Seated at one of the park benches were two fine gentlemen reunited after years apart—Professor Jurjik Sowenso and Doctor Shay Shahidi. The Hajari experts had spent countless hours in conversation with Goura, exploring Hajar, Labeth, and the other surviving core worlds of the ancient Hajari Kingdom. Learning about the past was a passion that each man would cherish, and they could not thank the guys enough for breaking the embargo on Hajari research.

Chuck and Dave carried their champagne glasses to a bench underneath a stone statue, content to watch the party from the sidelines on this gorgeous, sun-kissed day. The guys were kings of their own planet now, in a manner of speaking. They were trustees of the Paradise Collective—a legal entity comprising the guys, the Paradise Emissaries, and the living planet itself. They were also majority shareholders of Haven Resort Pty Ltd, and proud of it.

The statue behind them showed this relationship if one interpreted it that way. It showed five people—our intrepid band of star-travelling misfits, plus the distinguished Chief Emissary, Sequoia—reaching towards a globe, holding it up, supporting it. It was supposed to be symbolic of the teamwork and unity that helped rebuild Paradise after an unfortunate ecological disaster. That was the story told to every resort visitor and journalist who cared to ask.

But for the guys, the globe meant something else. It reminded them of how they managed to finance this dream of theirs. It reminded them of their struggle to find investors. And it reminded them of that fateful day when Jimmy, being Jimmy, whacked a tennis ball in an antique shop and, to appease the shop owner, bought a wooden box on impulse. The orb inside that box started them on a wild journey that not only brought them closer together but introduced them to wonderful friends who helped them achieve their dream.

They owed it all especially to Goura Ganna Grithl, otherwise known as King Gannik, the last ruler of the Hajari Kingdom.

APPENDIX

AN OVERVIEW OF THE HAJARI CIVIL WAR

Journal of Xenoarchaeology, Vol. 1035, No. 3

Jurjik Sowenso and **Shay Shahidi**
Galactic Institute of Xenology, University of Oxford

Summary: The disappearance of the Hajari Kingdom has been one of xenoarchaeology's greatest mysteries. For many years, the only evidence of the existence of this ancient civilisation was the devastated world of Akalam, some salvaged written material, a handful of artefacts, and two obscure orbs of malevolent design. Recent discoveries have finally shed light on the downfall of Hajari civilisation. Future research promises to fill the void of understanding that has existed for so long. Based on new primary evidence, this article is a starting point to understanding the final years of the once-great Hajari Kingdom.

THE KINGDOM

THE HAJARI KINGDOM INCLUDED seven Core Worlds and innumerable satellite colonies. The Core Worlds were each ruled by one of the offspring of the ruling king, and were known as principalities. According to the Royal Annals, the last sovereign of the Hajari Kingdom was King Roluth, his reign ending approximately in the Earth year of 855 CE.

The administrative capital of the kingdom was Hajar, recently discovered by the late independent xenoarchaeologist Count Karl Friedrich von Mein, who was killed while investigating the ruins of Fortress Milkha, King Roluth's residence. To preserve this archaeological site for study, the location of this planet remains top secret. However, the other six Core Worlds have also been discovered, as well as a growing number of colonies, and these will open for tours once they have been sufficiently excavated and studied.

The seven Core Worlds (written in their original names) and their rulers are:

- Hajar (capital) – Princess Arunath
- Heshwan – Prince Gannik
- Labeth – Prince Sharnek
- Tibiri – Princess Dakay
- Emeled – Prince Barshun
- Zanadab – Prince Illak
- Merus – Prince Vonar.

THE HAJARI ORBS

To understand the causes of the Civil War and the downfall of the Hajari Kingdom, one must understand the origins and purpose of the Hajari orbs. Towards the end of his reign, King Roluth created seven coloured orbs, perfectly spherical objects with immense power. Research has begun to determine the technological foundations of the orbs—a project that is proving more difficult than anticipated.

The orbs served several purposes. At the most basic level, they were symbols of power and authority. Each child of Roluth received an orb as follows:

- Yellow orb – Princess Arunath
- Green orb – Prince Gannik
- Pink orb – Prince Sharnek
- Blue orb – Princess Dakay
- Red orb – Prince Barshun
- Purple orb – Prince Illak
- Silver orb – Prince Vonar.

There is no order of precedence for orb ownership. All orbs were equal. In addition to being symbols of government, the orbs also acted as communication tools and tracking beacons. When coupled with the right communications apparatus, one orb user could contact another within the extremities of the kingdom. Each orb has a built-in beacon mechanism for inter-stellar tracking, again only within the boundaries of the kingdom and only usable with the appropriate supporting hardware.

An unsubstantiated claim is that the orbs were used as keys to King Roluth's private treasury. So far, no evidence has been found to support the existence of such a treasury. Despite this, Hajari treasures have been uncovered on each of the Core Worlds. The University of Oxford is in the process of negotiating the study and exhibition of these artefacts, as well as the auctioning of duplicate or surplus artefacts.

The most insidious purpose of the orbs has been left to last, because it is closely linked with the origin of the Civil War.

When coupled with its accompanying sceptre, an orb becomes a weapon of devastating destruction. Military use of the orbs resulted in the demise of the kingdom and the civilisation as a whole.

THE CIVIL WAR

THE HAJARI CIVIL WAR began shortly after King Roluth's death around Earth year 855 CE. The Royal Annals note that Roluth's chosen successor was Princess Arunath. However, Prince Vonar, her older brother, challenged the decision. This led to a brutal war between King Roluth's children. The Loyalists were led by Arunath, and she was supported by two of her brothers, Gannik and Sharnek, and her sister, Dakay. The Anti-Successionists were led by Vonar, with the support of the final two brothers, Illak and Barshun. Thus, the siblings fought for control of the kingdom.

The war devastated the Hajari worlds. Not only did it destroy cities and entire populations, but it also wreaked havoc on the planets themselves. Akalam, a colony for Outsiders (outcasts), is a perfect example of the destructive power of an orb. The planet's crust was shattered after repeated bombardment, leading to massive tectonic movements, continent-sized fissures, repeated volcanic eruptions, and permanent lava flows. While King Roluth's children battled for supremacy, the kingdom and its people suffered.

Records of the Civil War are scarce, perhaps because the civilisation ended either during it or soon after. This article now outlines the scant details of the final months of the Civil War.

258

The Anti-Successionist Prince Illak was the first to be executed. Arunath defeated him on Zanadab. There is evidence of Arunath using Illak's purple orb to fight during later battles, but a diary written by her chief of staff mentions Arunath sending the orb far away not long after the Battle of Zanadab. Count Mein and the writers of this article discovered Illak's purple orb in 3225 on an isolated planet called Revhou, located in the outer part of the Scutum Arm of the galaxy.

Following Illak's execution, the Anti-Successionist leader, Vonar, launched a renewed offensive against Loyalist forces, obliterating satellite colonies and conquering Core Worlds one after the other. Heshwan, the domain of Prince Gannik, buckled under Vonar's onslaught. Gannik himself was killed before Vonar moved on to Labeth. However, it seems Gannik hid his green orb among the stars, for it was discovered by Count Mein in 3228 at the bottom of a lake on Calcor, many lightyears from its home.

At Labeth, Vonar crushed Prince Sharnek, laying waste to the entire planet. Then, he moved on to Tibiri, where he defeated Princess Dakay. Her blue orb, like Gannik's and Illak's, disappeared from Hajari space, perhaps in an attempt to limit the power that Vonar was undoubtedly seeking. Dakay's blue orb was later discovered in 3235 on Isthan by James Jonathon Jones, an Earth-born tourist resort executive.

With four siblings dead, Princess Arunath now faced her brothers Vonar and Barshun alone. The battle that raged on Hajar ground the planet into dust, for the surface is now mostly desert. Notably, shells of important buildings still stand. The most important of these are the Palace of Majesty, from which Arunath would have governed Hajar before her ascension to the throne; and Fortress Milkha, from which King Roluth would have ruled the kingdom when he was still alive. It was here, in the administrative district, that the Hajari Kingdom took its last breath. The three surviving siblings fought wildly for a dying civilisation, and they themselves perished under the might of their own attacks.

CONCLUSION

THE DEATH OF ROLUTH's children brought an end to the Hajari Kingdom. Survivors of the war—of which there would have been few—were not equipped to repair the damage wrought by the royal siblings. Eventually, the inheritors of dead and dying worlds succumbed to the long-lasting effects of the world-destroying orbs. In time, the Hajari civilisation fell dormant and then lay in obscurity for over two thousand years.

As xenoarchaeologists flock to study the remains of this once-great civilisation, the ever-present reminder of death and destruction looms heavy over their heads. The best a xenoarchaeologist can do for a civilisation that suffered so much is to learn its history and record it for future generations. In the case of Hajari history, a xenoarchaeologist's prerogative is to ensure that the billions who perished can be remembered once again, and that the mistakes of the past are brought to light so they will not be repeated. To this end, the orbs and their sceptres remain the property of the University of Oxford and are kept in separate locations under heavy security.

ACKNOWLEDGEMENTS

I had always intended to write a sequel to *Space Trip*. However, crafting a science fiction comedy novel is harder than it sounds. A few people made the process easier. I thank my parents and my siblings for an unending source of humour. I also thank my editor, who helped me shape the story, and Tom Edwards for giving each of my main characters a face. But the highest praise goes to my readers—your interest in *Space Trip* encourages me to continue the series.

ABOUT THE AUTHOR

Nick Marone grew up in Sydney, Australia before eventually moving south towards Canberra. He developed an interest in science fiction in his teens and has been hooked ever since. His first book, the novella *Fire Over Troubled Water*, was released in 2019, and his first *Space Trip* book was published in 2022. Over the years, he has worked for *Aurealis* and *Andromeda Spaceways Magazine*.

You can follow Nick and subscribe to his free newsletter at **nickmarone.com**.

SPACE TRIP

Four friends—Dave, Eddie, Jimmy, and Chuck—are fed up with their boring lives. So when Eddie builds a personal interstellar space craft, the obvious thing is to go somewhere. Little do the guys know that simply going somewhere is never quite that easy. The galaxy is a big place, full of complex worlds, people of ill repute, and unexpected events popping up at the wrong time.

Join our woefully underprepared friends as they try desperately to get to the tourist world known as Paradise. Climb aboard *Liberty*, Eddie's oddly-shaped but perfectly functional ship, and share in their pains and joys as they press on to their goal and maybe learn a bit about themselves along the way. You deserve a break, too, and what better way to do so than to spend time with four misfits who clearly need help?

Chuck says to bring coffee when you meet them at the spaceport—don't forget!

Printed in Australia
AUHW021348251022
370677AU00009B/47

9 780648 864141